A Pocket Tour of Music on the Internet

Colin Berry

San Francisco • Paris • Düsseldorf • Soest   **SYBEX**

Pocket Tour Concept:	Brenda Kienan
Acquisitions Manager:	Kristine Plachy
Developmental Editor:	Brenda Kienan
Editor:	Abby Azrael
Technical Editor:	Michelle Moore
Book Designer and Desktop Publisher:	Emil Yanos
Graphic Artist:	Cuong Le
Production Assistant:	Alexa Riggs
Indexer:	Ted Laux
Cover Designer:	Joanna Kim Gladden
Cover Illustrator:	Mike Miller

Library of Congress Card Number: 95-68653

ISBN: 0-7821-1695-7

Manufactured in the United States of America

10 9 8 7 6 5 4 3 2 1

Acknowledgments

If every book is a journey, then *A Pocket Tour of Music on the Internet* took me to places I'd never imagined, and introduced me to some remarkable people along the way.

My thanks first to my editor, Abby Azrael, who—for better or worse—now knows me and our subject in great depth. When you write *your* first book, pray for an editor as good as Abby.

Thanks also to the people with whom I worked at Sybex: Brenda Kienan for her phone call, months ago, and·her developmental ideas; Dan Tauber for his endless patience; Michelle Moore for her technical know-how; Emil Yanos for designing and typesetting the book; Alexa Riggs for proofreading; and Cuong Le for transforming my cryptic scrawls into art.

I also want to thank Mark Frauenfelder, Carla Sinclair, and Eric Herbert for fielding my myriad questions (often asked in the dead of night) and continuing to call me their friend, and Gareth Branwyn for our two-hour conversation that led to this book. Thanks also to Ted Dively and Matt Wood for gently coaxing me over the Mac/PC hump.

Finally, thanks above all to the men and women who are bringing music to the Internet: Your hard work—often done for free—is what made this book possible.

Table of Contents

Introduction

So...why did you pick up this book?

Sorry—that's a pretty personal question, and we hardly know each other. But even though we haven't been introduced, I already know something about you: You probably own a computer, or at least work with one, and you're probably someone who's interested in music.

You might be a fan of the opera, or of a band who plays on MTV. Maybe you collect old blues records; maybe you're into the acid jazz scene. You may be a musician yourself—the guitarist for a country-western band or timpanist for a symphony orchestra. Maybe you're a rapper for an up-and-coming hip-hop act; maybe you're a music journalist.

I know something else about you, too: unless you've been living beneath a large rock, you've probably heard a lot about the Internet recently. And, whatever your musical connection, you're wondering: What will *A Pocket Tour of Music on the Internet* do for me?

I think this book will do a lot for you, and I'll try to explain why.

Technology and music have worked side by side since before the invention of the gramophone, and the Internet—a communication tool like the telephone, a media source like a newspaper, a news and entertainment hub like TV—marks the next logical step in that partnership.

As the central tool for a world becoming increasingly digital, the Internet is emerging as a crucial place to turn for business, educational, or leisure-time needs, a place where technology collaborates with particular interests. Some people are interested in plugging in—or, as they often say, *jacking in*—to the Net in order to trade stocks, others to conduct university research, still others to chat with their friends.

You're interested in connecting to the Internet for another reason altogether: You enjoy music, and want to use the Net to expand your interest in it—to track down musical information, read reviews, to see pictures of your favorite artists, maybe even listen to a song or two. With that in mind, you picked up this book.

WHO THIS BOOK IS FOR

A Pocket Tour of Music on the Internet is designed for someone just like you—a computer user who's also an aficionado of music.

This book presumes three basic things about you: You're comfortable working on a PC, you like music, and you want to find it on the Internet—and that's all. It's neither a particularly technical nor an overly simplistic book, but rather a detailed guidebook to finding the great music available on the Net.

And it *is* there. Believe me.

While ideally suited for someone who has little or no Internet experience—I was new to the medium myself, not so long ago—*A Pocket Tour of Music on the Internet* will also satisfy the savvy, seasoned Net-surfer and all those in between.

As a fan of music first and a computer enthusiast second, I'm going to offer a particular perspective on our subject—music on the Internet. Within these pages, I'm not going to tell you that the Net is a perfect place, or that you're *riding the wave of the future*, or that the Net will replace other media or communications methods—I don't think it will. I do believe, however, that the Net will eventually be *just as viable* a tool or medium as TV, radio, and the daily newspaper—it may even prove as useful as the telephone some day.

So why not jack in now and get comfortable? And why not discover some great music to listen to while you're settling in?

WHAT'S IN THIS BOOK?

I've designed this *Pocket Tour* to maximize your enjoyment of music in this remarkable new electronic multimedium. Part One, "The Basics," walks you through the fundamentals you'll need to successfully connect to the Internet and enjoy some of its basic resources—the mailing lists, newsgroups, file transfer sites, and stops on the World Wide Web.

You'll learn what hardware and software you need to start, how to set it all up correctly, and how to connect to the Internet. You'll learn some basic searching and downloading software programs, standard applications that you'll use online, some lingo, and some Netiquette. You'll be amazed at how easy it is to familiarize yourself with the Net.

Part Two, "The Sites," is a smorgasbord of music-related Internet stops, all fully accessible using the simple skills you'll learn in Part One. In this second part, you'll find hundreds of sites where you can do everything from subscribing to a mailing list for bass guitar players to downloading a sample of Schubert. You'll discover very quickly that your *Pocket Tour* is the essential guide to finding just what you want, be it a newsgroup for Latin dance music or a site with files of R.E.M. lyrics.

HOW TO USE THIS BOOK

Just like a guidebook you take along when visiting an unfamiliar city, your *Pocket Tour* is the perfect companion to your travels on the Internet.

If you're new to the Internet, you'll probably rely first on Part One, orienting yourself before plunging into the many entries found in Part Two. If you're already computer- and Internet-savvy, you'll find Part Two immediately helpful, and may return to Part One to refresh your skills for a particular activity. Whichever approach you use, you'll find your *Pocket Tour* a valuable guide to getting the musical most of the Internet.

In "The Basics," you'll find it most effective to read linearly, reading Notes, Tips, and Warnings (each marked with a specific icon, which we'll discuss in just a moment) in the order in which they're presented, and noting any shaded sections in context with their surrounding subjects. Because it's the how-to section of the book, Part One builds on information you've learned throughout its pages, delivering you to the Internet with a working knowledge of what to do there. Read Part One straight through, just as you would any instruction manual.

In Part Two, "The Sites," you'll probably find it most effective to begin with a music genre that interests you, from Alternative to Folk, from Rock to Classical,and from Jazz, R & B, and Rap to International. Once there, you can easily jump around *within* categories (choosing among several jazz artists, for example) or *across* them (tracking down, say, a mailing list you found in a record company's newsgroup), chasing down particular subjects in whatever way you like. If you're not sure where to begin within a genre, you'll often find Notes that indicate my suggested starting places. Since all the genres and entries found in Part Two are accessible with equal ease using the information you'll learn in "The Basics," you can't go wrong in any direction.

Because it's a guidebook first and foremost, I recommend having your *Pocket Tour* open on the desk while you cruise online, feeling free to mark its pages with additional notes and updated information.

CONVENTIONS USED IN THIS BOOK

To help you get around its pages, your *Pocket Tour* makes use of several tools and navigational devices that aid you in better understanding your subject.

 This icon indicates Notes you may find useful while reading—additional information, interesting asides, and points of greater detail.

 This icon indicates Tips that will help you in your online connection or travels, highlighting key points that may get you connected faster or more efficiently.

 This icon signifies a point of Warning; it asks you to stop and carefully consider a critical moment or a process that may go wrong.

The following icons mark the types of entries found in Part Two:

 indicates a Mailing List

 indicates a Newsgroup

 indicates an FTP site

 indicates a site on the World Wide Web

Don't worry if you don't know the difference between (or have never even heard of) these types of entries; Part One explains each of them very clearly. This last icon is used occasionally:

 This marks my personal picks from the entries in Part Two— sites whose superb content, colorful layout, or hospitable atmosphere deserve special mention. The sites with this icon mark the best I found in cyberspace, and you'll find several in each genre section.

TUNING UP, TAKING OFF

Your *Pocket Tour of Music on the Internet* is the first of its kind, a guidebook that marries two seemingly divergent subjects—music and the Internet. The book reflects research and writing done while the Net is still growing like a spring flower (or an unruly adolescent), when music on the Net is just beginning to become widely available.

Although I've designed this book for minimum confusion and maximum enjoyment, you should understand that our medium is one in which things change with unbelievable swiftness. Sites up and running today could—occasionally—be gone tomorrow; conversely, a hundred new sites may have sprung up overnight. Use this guidebook as a way to get you to one of the fastest moving and most awe-inspiring places on the planet, a place where Debussy and Dylan convert to digits, where anyone with a little know-how and the right machinery can discover a remarkable musical world.

Are you with me? Let's go!

Part One:
The Basics

What Is the Internet?

What is this thing we call the Internet? Easily the most talked-about cultural phenomenon of this decade, the Internet seems to be where the world wants to go: People as diverse as the Speaker of the U.S. House of Representatives to members of Van Halen are jumping on the Internet for a piece of the online action, to stake a claim on this remarkable new multimedium. We constantly hear the term tossed around the media, but no one really stops to define it. Just what *is* the Internet?

Technically, the Internet is an intricate web of PCs and mainframes connected via phone lines and modems—a global network of networks and single computers. But that technical definition makes the Internet sound too tangled, when in fact it's a brilliantly woven fabric spun by thousands of intercommunicating computers.

A series of better questions might be: What is the Internet *for me*? A gathering of minds? A tool to help people? A resource for experts? A sophisticated toy for the general public?

You guessed it: The Internet is all those. And more.

TODAY'S INTERNET

To say the Internet is expanding is the ultimate understatement; *exploding* is a more accurate description. The Internet adds an estimated ten to twenty percent more users—something like a hundred thousand new members—to its ranks every month, though no one knows exactly how many users jack in for the first time in a given month. In the first year it became available, the World Wide Web, a particular section of the Internet, saw an increase in its traffic of 341,634 percent.

The Net's exponential expansion is a good thing on several counts. First, the increase in users results in an ever-expanding group of pooled resources: The Net is a collective gathering of brains, electronic and human, and the more gray matter there is behind the keyboards, the smarter the Net becomes. Second, as the Net begins to appeal to an increasingly broad range of users, it becomes easier and easier for the common human—that's you and me—to use. Finally, no matter how big it gets, the Net will always serve all the users who choose to jack in. The Internet isn't like an island where unchecked growth is eventually dangerous: Still marked with the same fiercely independent spirit with which it began, the Internet is expanding as a medium without boundaries.

 The U.S. has always understood the vitality of a nation's communications network: One of our goals in the Gulf war was to disable Iraq's "command and control structure"—in other words, the Iraqi Internet.

It's important to note that currently, and probably for eternity, no central organization runs the Internet. The Internet is run on thousands of computers—mainframes and PCs alike—and by millions of users; its strength is in this patchwork design, each computer contributing a single accessible thread.

This fabric woven of tiny filaments makes for the Net's best and worst characteristics. On the bad side, some threads are delicate: Any one of the machines on that grid may be unplugged, understaffed, or overused. As a music fan, you'll occasionally find you want to access a *site*—a particular place on the Internet—that's temporarily down or too busy to service you. Sometimes you can default to a *mirror site*—a back-up location that carries the same info—sometimes you can't. It can be frustrating.

But the advantage to this patchwork system is that its individual components provide the best source for detail and minutiae, a goldmine of specificity and particular use. Once you have found that source for rare vinyl Perez Prado back-catalogues you heard existed, you couldn't be happier.

Such a system, a tapestry woven of millions of single threads, fosters a remarkable spirit of community, one that counteracts your potential for loneliness. While the absence of a central organization means that initially you surf the Net alone, you'll find colleagues and fellow Netizens extremely willing to assist you, either by explaining what you don't understand or letting you in on techniques that have helped them. With everyone being equal on the Net, the only competition seems to be in racing to discover something first, coming back to tell everyone, and watching them scramble to get there and check it out themselves.

THE FUTURE OF THE NET

What will the future hold for the Net? With slick and friendly applications like Mosaic, a program for World Wide Web that organizes text in a whole new way, or the remarkable viewing and listening capabilities you'll find available via FTP (which we'll talk about very soon), the Net stands poised to spring into the new millennium with user-friendly screens, faster operating speeds, and universal accessibility. The size of the Internet may level off, but the quality of its technology will not. Internet enthusiasts from engineers to home tinkerers will continue seeking ways to improve the existing system, to speed it up or render the images and files gathered from it in greater detail, to expand or tighten its focus.

The Internet's Dark History

A relic of the cold war, the Internet began in the late 1960s as part of an experiment by the U.S. Department of Defense (DOD) to link research computers for its Advanced Research Projects Agency (ARPA) at labs across the country. In those days, two or more computers that were *networked*—cabled to communicate back and forth—had to be directly plugged into one another using a one-to-one linking system, the networked computers trading data in one steady, single-file stream.

Desiring a utility more efficient than this direct-line method, the DOD sought to nationally network its computers using a faster and more efficient "highway" system, whereby *packets*—gathered, disassembled, sent, and reassembled chunks of information—would travel a common path on their route to the receiving computer. The DOD designed this new system, called ARPAnet, to remain up and running even if particular circuits, stations, or labs weren't working. Why wouldn't they be working? The DOD, while seeking a reliable national computer network, also wanted a fail-safe system in the event of, and in preparation for, nuclear attack. They needed a grid built of multiple links in case any were bombed out of existence.

That nuclear war, you may recall, never came. Ironically, though, this massive computer network designed for fail-safe military use has transmogrified into one of the century's most successful public communications systems. ARPAnet has become the Internet, a rock-solid "internetwork" available to thousands of large and small local and national computer systems, as well as millions of American and international users who daily enjoy the fruits of the DOD's labor. Replacing a-bombs with e-mail, the Internet stands as the ultimate sword-turned-ploughshare, a testament to the remarkable transformation that can come of doomsday technology.

As a music aficionado, I predict that we've only begun to exploit the Internet and its capabilities as an archive and information tool. Data of all types will continue to proliferate with ever-increasing availability, diversity, detail, and speed. Even in the time I spent preparing this book, I found software and navigation tools improving, varieties of available music widening, and increasing numbers of library-sized musical archives. I also added dozens of entries to the book as I went along: Record companies, promoters, fan clubs, and musical services. I can only imagine what will happen in the next five years.

I think it's important to get involved with the Net now because it's the best medium I've found that makes digital technology available for the everyday person; it's where the future lies. More than here to stay, the Net is here to change with the needs of its users, and while it won't replace television, telephone, or print media, it will become just as necessary. In its future, the Net will be just as crucial as any other form of communication to musicians, music businesspeople, professional performers, and weekend fans.

I recommend you acquaint yourself with this medium while it's still growing and developing, while its quirks still aren't quite ironed out. I recommend familiarizing yourself with its systems as they exist now, and then fastening your seatbelt: The Net at the turn of the century may improve as much from current standards as today's net has from 1970s ARPAnet. Wait and see....

What Do You Need to Cruise the Net?

I first surfed the Internet on an old Macintosh computer with a tiny black-and-white monitor and a sluggish constitution, quickly realizing that although I could do a few basic functions—read my e-mail, chat with people, scan my newsgroups (which you'll learn how to access shortly)—I was enjoying only a fraction of what the Internet had to offer.

Interfaces—the screens where I did my work at various Internet stops—were plain and ugly. I couldn't really *download* or *upload*—transfer data from another computer onto mine or from mine to another—because I didn't have the storage space. When I did download, it took forever because I had a snail-paced modem. As my blood pressure and my phone and credit card bills crept progressively higher, I swore to upgrade my equipment.

If you're like I was, you'll need some basics to cruise the Net, but you need not spend a fortune.

HARDWARE

This probably won't come as a shock: You need a computer first and foremost to cruise the Internet, and you need an efficient one. I don't mean expensive, but you'll need one that has plenty of memory and whose working speed is fast enough for you to tolerate.

You need a computer that won't (like the lover in that popular song) drive you crazy. A standard-issue PC running Windows, a color monitor, plenty of available RAM (which I'll also talk more about in a minute), and a fast-working hard drive are all crucial to your comfort. I'm not advocating mounting a huge debt to guarantee your enjoyment on the Internet, but without this basic hardware, you'll be miserable. And no one should be miserable in such a remarkable place.

Your keenest strategy for getting the best hardware while keeping costs to a minimum is to be informed: Read those computer-centered magazines, newspapers, and books, and familiarize yourself with the most current data surrounding Net equipment. Keep abreast of whose hardware is immediately outdated and whose software programs are on the cutting edge.

Besides your computer, you also need a way to connect to the Internet. If you work in a computerized office, you may already have Internet access; ask your technical support person if the network you work on is connected to the Internet. In some cities, a new kind of connection, called Integrated Services Digital Network (ISDN), uses an adapter box—much like your cable TV hook-up—that provides a high-speed connection to the Net. The most common way to connect a stand-alone PC is by using a *modem*—an accessory that connects your machine to a phone line and you to the Internet.

Modems used to be strictly *external*—separate components plugged in to your *modem port*. But because PC users find using them increasingly desirable, modems (moda?) are increasingly *internal*—i.e., already built in to your computer. Many PC packages come bundled with one. Whether internal or external, a modem is one essential link between your PC and everything that's out there in cyberspace.

If you're using a modem to connect to the Internet, get a good one. I've heard good things about Supra and Cardinal products, as well as Practical Peripherals. To conform to industry standards, your modem needs to support a v.32bis *method of transmission (and* v.42bis *will soon be a must); it also must be* Hayes *compatible.*

Once your modem connects your PC to its destination, it's also the tool that transfers data to and from that site, a task the modem should perform at a very high speed. A modem's data-transfer rate is measured in *bps*—bits per second. The faster its bps rate, the less Net-time your modem will spend transferring files.

A few years ago, most modems transferred data at a standard speed of 2400 bps. These days, however, anything slower than 14,400 bps hinders your enjoyment on the Internet.

Some cybersystems can't yet run (reliably, at least) at the fastest speeds. I currently use a 14,400 bps (a.k.a. 14.4 kpbs, or *kilo*bits per second) modem, but several of my regular connections (my online service provider and two bulletin board systems I haunt) don't support that particular speed, and must run at a slower 9600 bps. Because you can always run a faster modem at slower speeds by altering its settings when you dial a particular connection, however, I still recommend purchasing the fastest modem you can afford—a 28.8 kbps or faster, ideally.

A basic computer with a supercharged modem is many times preferable to a top-of-the-line computer with a lethargic modem. Trust me; I've tried both.

I need to mention two other hardware options: First, because you'll be running many different applications while on the Internet, and because you'll frequently want to download large files, your computer should have plenty of memory available—not less than 4MB of RAM, I'd say—earmarked strictly for Net use. That means if, like me, you're running a computer that already needs about 4MB of memory to run its operating system, you may need to double it. A memory upgrade may sound like an added headache, but I promise you'll be happier having extra memory rather than not enough. Imagine how frustrated you'll be, for example, if you stumble across a remarkable audio or graphics file in a hard-to-access site but don't have enough RAM to hold it. If you don't invest in that additional 4MB, it's a likely scenario. The extra cost will be worth every penny in the long run.

Second, in this book in particular and in any discussion of music on the Internet, you will hear much about a *soundcard*—a necessary strip of internal hardware that, once installed in your PC, not only enables you to play audio files directly from your computer, but—using compression, enhanced stereo capabilities, and other technnology—drastically improves the sound quality of those files. To play back music gathered from the Internet, a PC *must* have a soundcard, whether it comes with the computer or is installed later.

These days, because so many individuals and businesses demand them, dealers sell many new PCs already bundled with excellent soundcards.

Currently, it takes a lot of work to listen to music on the Internet: After securing a soundcard, the devotee must locate the audio file, download it (a process that can take fifteen to twenty minutes for a three-minute sound clip, depending on your modem's speed), decompress the file with the appropriate software, store it (a process that uses a huge amount of RAM), and download its *playback*—listening—software before he or she can listen to a single byte of music. That's too bad: I want to be the first to hear about systems that are easier to work with than the existing one.

 Speaking of which, here's my e-mail address: cpberry@aol.com. *If you write, let me know what you liked about* A Pocket Tour of Music on the Internet *and if there's anything I've left out or made unclear.*

SOFTWARE

You already know that the fastest and finest hardware available is useless without smart software to power it. To cruise the Internet you'll need a variety of applications, from programs that get you there to many you'll need for browsing once you're online.

The first program you'll need to begin your journey into the Internet is the *communications* software that operates your modem. If you've just bought an external modem, you'll need to install these applications on your hard disk. Since PCs with internal modems generally come with their communications software already installed, you'll need to search your hard disk (or consult your owner's manual) to track it down.

This software enables your computer to locate its modem and prepare it for dialing out, to register many computer products by phone, to reach bulletin board systems (BBSs) and other networks, and, on some systems, to send and receive faxes. Your modem software allows you to access the Internet and view, hear, and transfer the documents you find there.

Second, you'll need those applications that get you up and running online, programs that initiate the sophisticated hardware-handshaking between your computer and your *Internet service provider*—the company that provides your connection to the Internet. In most cases, your Internet service provider will mail you this startup software upon receiving your initial fees.

The third group of applications you'll need are the three programs described in the "Software 101" sections of this part: Gopher, some kind of FTP application, and a browser for the World Wide Web. These common programs are available as Net freeware and should be easy to find.

Fourth, since cover art, promotional press, and digitized images are more and more available to music fans on the Internet, you'll also probably want software to view graphics files. JPEG, GIF (for specific definitions of these and other terms, see "Lingo," later in this part), and other viewing applications

Trumpets, Chameleons, and WinSocks: What's It All About?

For PCs using a particular connection called *SLIP* or *PPP*—a common type of Internet link that you'll soon learn much more about—you'll need two additional items on your hard drive: WinSock, a library of commands and procedures that (among other things) standardizes the communication between your machine and others, and either Chameleon Sampler or Trumpet, applications that support WinSock. Whew!

WinSock is a *DLL*—Dynamic Link Library, the translating link between what are called *TCP/IP*—the languages computers on the Internet use to speak to one another. For more information about Internet protocols, see "SLIP/PPP Access Providers," discussed later in this part.

Some service providers may give you just a telephone number to dial, presuming that you already have the necessary software for connecting to, and navigating, the Internet. If that's your case, they're presuming you have WinSock and Chameleon Sampler or Trumpet, WinSock's supporting programs.

Chameleon Sampler and Trumpet are available from several sources: You can download them from the Internet; you can purchase one of many books that have them bundled in the back; you

Chameleon Sampler gives you point-and-click access to many Net programs.

usually are available from the same site where you find the file itself. Many new computers come with such applications already installed.

Fifth and finally, because you've chosen this particular book, there's a good chance you'll want to listen to the music you find on the Internet. If you do, you'll also need software that allows you to play back the sound and video files you've chosen to download. Like viewing applications, most playback programs are available from or near the same sites where you downloaded the music files themselves. Make sure you have a soundcard installed on your machine.

I heard that collective moan: What?? "Shell Account??" "TCP?" "IP?" "SLIP?" "PPP?" Is this one of those technobabble books? Nope. Keep reading. You'll understand those terms—and many others—sooner than you think.

You'll see terms like .WAV, .MID, .MOD, .AU, or others that refer to the different types of music files. Think of these *extensions*—suffixes to filenames

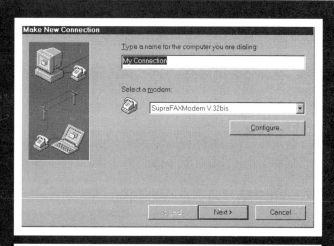

Windows 95 Remote Access makes access to the Internet a breeze.

can also get them from many Internet service providers who provide a copy of one on disk when you sign up.

A disclaimer: If you or the company you work for use a *shell account*—a connection that utilizes the Unix operating system, which relies on typed commands for navigation—you may not need any of these applications. If your office has a central computer system, ask your technical department if you can already access the Internet.

Whatever your case, you can get all the software needed to access the Net from Windows 95, using its Remote Access program to call up a service provider and connect to the Internet using SLIP or PPP (see "Internet Service Providers," discussed later in this part).

that indicate the type of file—as different formats, each requiring its own type of player (see Figure 1.1). For a full listing of audio file formats and their conversions, see ".AU, .AIFF, .AIFC, .AAAAGH!" in the "Special Collectors' Section" of Part Two.

Until music files are standardized, my suggestion to those readers seeking listenable music is to wait until you find a file in a particular format before downloading its playback application. Once you find that rare P-Funk WAV file, chances are you can locate a WAV player right next door. Be patient.

Remember what I said earlier about having plenty of memory available?

Once you're online, much of this necessary software will be available to you. If you need a current copy of Gopher, FTP and similar programs, or a

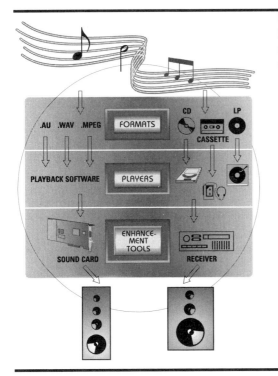

Figure 1.1:
Different types of playback files are similar to different listening formats: CDs, cassettes, and LPs.

World Wide Web browser, for example (see "Lingo" for definitions of these terms), you usually can find it in cyberspace. Likewise, upgraded versions of Trumpet and Chameleon programs often can be found on the Net. Although you can find freeware and shareware programs for almost everything you want to do, you may need to purchase some applications from a software vendor.

Freeware *are free programs available in the public domain;* shareware *applications are available for copying, but require you, if you end up using the program, to pay its author a reasonable fee. Both are available on the Internet.*

This book offers hundreds of suggested stops for touring the musical Internet, but I compiled its listings using exactly the same applications you'll learn about in the "Software 101" sections of this part. Designers have come up with remarkable applications whose ability to gather information can outdo any book, particularly when you're seeking a subject as fluid as "music on the Internet." Use your *Pocket Tour* as a guidebook that works hand-in-mouse with this smart software to direct you to those first stops. From there, let your imagination take over. . . .

Internet Service Providers

Besides proper hardware and software, you also need, before you get started, a connection to the Internet—something you can't achieve without a middleman. If you're a university student, you may have Internet access through your department's computer lab; if you're an employee of a company with an existing computer network, you may have access to some or all of the Net's services. More and more commonly, you may be a private user employing what's called a SLIP or PPP connection (two terms mentioned earlier and discussed shortly) to hook your stand-alone PC at your home or office to the Internet.

The middleman who makes these connections possible is your *Internet service provider*—any one of many companies whose business is to bring people like you or your university or company online. These service providers offer accounts for a wide range of users, from the weekend Net-surfer needing a modem-based connection to the largest corporate client who wants a permanent link to the Net.

Depending on your budget, your initial Internet connection can cost between $25 for a stand-alone PC and $6000 for an always-on link! Most connections, however, will cost you less than $50.

If you've checked in the back of any computer magazine lately, you probably know that these proliferating service providers—like hair salons, auto repair shops, law firms, or any other companies that serve the public—offer a variety of services for a variety of prices. (Some offer more for your money than others.)

Some provide connections designed for computer-savvy clients who don't mind using Unix commands to navigate the Internet; for the less experienced customer, other companies provide point-and-click Internet access. Some offer *e-mail* or *newsgroups*—two standard services that you'll learn about in "What Can I Do On the Internet?"—and little else, while others—the best of the bunch—offer complete Internet access (for an explanation, see "The Internet Shopping List" in this part).

If you're already connected to the Internet at your school or office, but you're not sure how much Net access you have, proceed directly to your department's tech person and ask. You'll be only the fiftieth person who's done so this month.

If you're lucky enough to have full Internet access through your workstation or university department, you can jump ahead at this point. Be warned, however, that many businesses frown on their employees using company computers (and company time) to cruise the Net; you can fritter away an hour with scarcely a blink.

Since switching companies is as easy as making a telephone call and programming a new number into your software, providers have found themselves in an incredibly competitive market. Reliably delivering your Internet needs while remaining essentially invisible, your provider should not only supply you the services you need and want, it should also be flexible.

You may begin, for example, wanting more direct applications and fewer fancy graphics. You may find you need only e-mail and never utilize FTP (my condolences!). You may initially have no interest in the World Wide Web, but find that later you become interested. Your needs will change over time on the Net, and your chosen service provider should reflect them. The service you choose must do many things for you: Shop around before committing, and make sure your company provides full Internet access when you do.

SHELL ACCOUNTS

People who already do much of their regular work on computers are likely to access the Internet using a shell account, which, you'll remember, is a connection based on the Unix operating system that relies on the user's typed commands for navigation. Currently the most common type of Internet connection, shell accounts are commonplace in computer-industry workstations, government offices, and university computer labs. BBSs and some employers' networks often utilize shell accounts as well.

Netcom's "Host" is a typical shell account that offers the small business or personal user FTP, Telnet (a system that allows you to access a remote computer), NetNews (a newsgroup application), and e-mail at low rates. They're nice people at Netcom, and seem willing to answer even the simplest questions.

The Internet Shopping List

A n Internet service provider should be your means to the online world, not an end in itself. These days, most companies provide most options on the Net, but here's a shopping list of your *minimum* needs:

◆ e-mail capability

◆ access to newsgroups (also called Usenet discussion groups)

◆ Gopher or WAIS information-searching systems

◆ *FTP*—File Transfer Protocol—a system for (surprise!) transferring files

◆ access to the World Wide Web (referred to interchangeably as *the Web* or *WWW*) which you'll view with a *browser*

(Please note that all these terms receive lengthy discussion in the "What Can I Do on the Internet?" section that follows.)

Optimally, your service provider should offer all of these options—*full Internet access*—with your account.

The appeal of a shell account is that as long as you know Unix, you're limited only by your system's access to the Internet. The disadvantage, however, is that your sole method of communication is typing, typing, and more typing. With a shell account, you can run a graphical program—a browser, say, for WWW—but you must launch it separately, and only if your provider offers access to (using that example) the Web itself.

If you're a devotee of Unix's simple elegance, I defer to your preferences, but shell accounts, for my dollar, are the least appealing way to connect to the Internet. I imagine plenty of well-qualified Unix-perts secretly join new users in welcoming the readily available and user-friendly graphic interfaces (see "Point-and-Click Accounts," later in this part).

Whether or not you work from a command-line interface, you may occasionally need to know a few Unix commands. Don't panic: See "Unix, Schmunix," which walks the inexperienced user through a basic set of them.

Watch for a program called TIA—*The Internet Adapter—that purports to transform a shell account into one that temporarily supports graphical programs. It may prove to be the big equalizer between connection methods.*

COMMERCIAL SERVICES

Offering e-mail delivery, network news, forums, as well as electronic magazines and newspapers, the commercial services—America Online, CompuServe, Prodigy, GEnie, Delphi, and eWorld—are becoming a common way to connect online. Home to thousands of users, they provide a supermarket of features (see Figure 1.2). They constantly improve interfaces and formats, and usually provide their customers with upgraded versions free of charge. Some rely on a command line to get around, but most employ simple point-and-click interfaces for navigation and are ideal for less experienced users.

To their credit, the commercial services seem willing to take an amateur by the mouse and guide him or her through the extras they offer; they're also quick to fix things that go wrong. But their sheer size makes these companies slow and clumsy at times. They tend to experience problems related to high traffic volume on their networks; their programs are occasionally incredibly slow, particularly when they're downloading a snazzy new icon or loading up your mail.

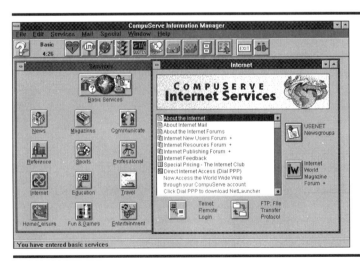

Figure 1.2:
CompuServe offers a wide range of options and services on its main menu.

In one sense, commercial services *are* Internet service providers—You can often access much of what the Internet offers through them. But if the true definition of the Internet encompasses everything that's available in cyberspace, then these companies, despite their user-friendly interfaces, are still quite limited. While you can buy and sell merchandise, ask computer-related questions, and look for romance on the services, you still can't get full Internet access: Some, for example, currently cannot deliver you to the WWW, although many plan to be able to do so very soon.

If the commercial services appeal to you, I'd recommend going ahead and starting with one; make note, however, of what frustrates you about it; a local SLIP/PPP provider may be able to address these problems for you.

SLIP/PPP ACCESS PROVIDERS

Let's talk about SLIP and PPP, something I've been alluding to since the "Software" section. To understand this efficient type of Internet link, you must first know that the Net is founded on basic *protocols*—sets of electronic conventions or formats (we called them "languages" earlier) that Internet computers must agree upon before successfully intercommunicating. These protocols—called TCP (*Transmission Control Protocol*) and IP (*Internet Protocol*)—enable your computer to temporarily communicate with others on the Internet.

Think of TCP/IP as similar to the requirements for sending a personal letter. For a domestic letter to successfully reach its addressee, the sender must follow some basic conventions: He or she must use an acceptable envelope (not too big or too small) with the address correctly positioned on it (on the front; name, address, and ZIP code) and the correct postage attached (using U.S. stamps, thank you). Following those basic regulations ensures that the letter reaches its intended reader.

Likewise, the Internet uses a similar set of conventions—the protocols mentioned above—that Internet computers need to agree on to successfully connect. Technically, SLIP and PPP are themselves protocols (*Serial Line Internet Protocol* and *Point-to-Point Protocol*, since you asked) that allow your PC to run its own applications on the Internet.

For the purposes of this book, however, SLIP and PPP are also the fastest-growing ways to get online. By enlisting with a local Internet access provider

Point-and-Click Accounts

Let's recap what's been said about Internet access so far: Most (though not all) commercial services offer friendly interfaces for easier navigation and plenty of extras, but don't offer the full oeuvre of Internet access. Some (though not all) shell accounts provide full Internet access, but require knowledge of the Unix command-line operating system. This chair is too hard, said Goldilocks; this one is too soft.

Do you see where this is heading?

One alternative many service providers offer to the Unix shell is an access method that, like the online services, uses a graphical interface. Netcom's successful "NetCruiser" account is such a system: From its point-and-click screen, NetCruiser allows you to switch among its windows to download files, read e-mail and newsgroups, and browse the WWW. It is but one of several access methods that deliver you to the Internet in its entirety using an interface designed for the average PC user.

who uses what's called a *SLIP connection* or *PPP connection*, many recently-wired PC users are finding an inexpensive and extremely efficient way to reach the Internet using just a modem and a telephone line. SLIP and PPP offer both full Internet access *and* user-friendly interfaces at relatively low cost.

This chair, said Goldilocks, is just right.

 What's the difference between SLIP and PPP? Technically, very little. PPP supposedly gives you more flexibility, but for all intents and purposes, consider SLIP and PPP to be the same thing. From this point on, I'll refer to them interchangeably as SLIP/PPP.

Using SLIP/PPP offers two advantages: First, it provides a temporary Internet link, perfect for the stand-alone PC, at a fraction of what a permanent hook-up would cost; SLIP/PPP essentially fools your computer (at least during the time it's connected) into thinking it's a full-time Internet machine (see Figure 1.3). Second, SLIP/PPP allows you to access the Internet using those programs and interfaces you're already familiar with, such as Microsoft Windows. Using SLIP/PPP is like purchasing standing-room opera tickets: With full access to raw Internet, you enjoy all the benefits of the featured performance, but with lower costs. And (unlike the opera) you actually get to sit down.

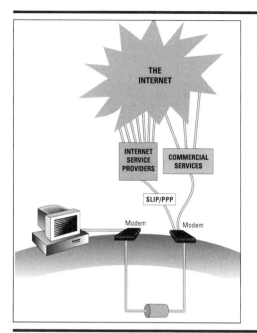

Figure 1.3:
SLIP/PPP uses familiar interfaces to deliver you to a fully accessible Internet.

There's no question that establishing SLIP/PPP is a little intimidating for the Net novice. It takes some real work to get things set up. I myself appreciated a little coaching when I first tiptoed around the Net, but with SLIP/PPP you're often expected to know many of the fundamentals on your own. Like so many things in the world, however, you pay much less if you know how to do a little more.

Say, for example, you want to transfer files. Whereas a commercial service may provide you the needed applications to do that with the click of an icon, SLIP/PPP requires you to run your own software. You must get ahold of those programs (either by purchasing or legally downloading them), correctly install them onto your computer, and know how to apply them. When you're employing SLIP/PPP, you have to run your own show.

While commercial services and some Unix accounts place limits on what you can do on the Internet, allowing you to run only software that their connection supports, SLIP/PPP gives you the flexibility to run *any* Internet programs you want (many of which are available as freeware or shareware) from your own PC, and at drastically lower costs. SLIP/PPP requires more tinkering, but your Net result is remarkable freedom.

It might seem, from a new user's standpoint, that to access your first versions of Net software you must already be familiar with the Net itself. Think about it: You've just arrived online, and you're seeking download information, but you need downloading software to get to it. Hel-lo? Can you say "Catch-22?"

I would suggest, here and at occasional confusing times when you're learning about the Internet, that you ask for help from your acquaintances. Buy the company computer geek or an online colleague a pizza after work and ask for a crash course on the Net. Chances are good that that person has access to freeware programs he or she can copy for you, or will be willing to help you cruise the Net to find your own. Ask people: They'll probably be proud to show you what they know. You'll spend quality time with people, get set up on the Internet, and learn something.

Keep the pizza off your PC's keyboard!

Internet access is a buyer's market right now. As an incentive to subscribe, many service providers offer introductory classes to their local customers, particularly in areas of the country where providers are sprouting like spring flowers. Another avenue for help would be to ask any potential provider about *support*—classes, technical help (both online and before you get there), and in-home service—when you're shopping around. Don't hesitate to demand the most for your money.

What about those package deals, the all-in-one start-up kits? You might try one, but remember that the Internet is subtle, complicated, and confusing at times. Cruising it can't be accomplished via "minute-to-learn/lifetime-to-master" instructions; it requires skills such as concentration, perseverance, patience, and intuition.

If you think you'll need a little coaching, I would try this approach: Sign on to a recommended commercial service that offers some Internet access. Poke around for a month, making mistakes, freezing your machine, getting frustrated, finding success. Whenever you have questions, ask—at the 1-800 numbers or online technical help your service provides, at computer stores, at gatherings of friends who work online. Once you become familiar with the medium, consider enlisting a full-access Internet provider.

Costs

I heard that question from the shy one in the back: How much will gaining access to the Internet cost you?

Not much: A PC with the standard DOS/Windows operating system, one with at least 8MB of RAM and that moves at a tolerably fast speed, is more than enough hardware to get you started. How much you spend on such hardware, or whether such specifications are crucial, is up to you. Windows 95 systems have more than enough power and flexibility to use on the Internet, but plenty of ancient machines run perfectly well too. In any case, a beefed-up old computer is far better than a shiny new one with no memory. To begin, spend as much as you need for a few basics to keep you satisfied, both on and off the Internet.

Like so many goods in the computer industry, modems are dropping in price while simultaneously achieving greater efficiency. You can pick up a high-quality 14.4 kbps modem for less than $100 now, and even the faster 28.8 kbps models—which may soon be the industry standard—don't cost much more than twice that.

Often, for a fraction of the original price, you can pick up a perfectly adequate modem from someone who's upgrading. As long as it's fast and designed for your machine and runs at 14.4 kbps or faster, it should work just fine. A modem that's "almost" right, however, will reveal its limitations at the most inopportune moment, and may save you no money at all.

Other costs to consider: As of this writing, a 4MB memory upgrade sells for about $150, plus tax, installation charges, and (if you buy through the mail) delivery—a bargain. You'll never have too much memory for your on-line travels.

PC soundcards start at $69 and shoot quickly skyward. If you intend to listen to music on the Internet, you must have one, so buy whatever's best for you. Music files on the Internet range from medium-quality monophonic to

8-bit stereo files, and, although I have yet to find any with the quality of audio CDs, music files can sound quite good once run through a sophisticated soundcard. The best soundcards have 16-bit stereo enhancing capabilities, which will be worth the investment if you end up listening to CD-ROMs or audio CDs through them.

Can we get technical for a minute? If you're an audio junkie looking to create the best sound quality from your PC, check out wavetable soundcards, *which offer even more realistic audio than the 16-bit stereo standards of most sound-cards. Well worth the money. We now return to our program in progress.*

You will have additional costs: Most Internet access providers charge one-time setup fees (in the $20 to $30 range for an individual customer) and an additional flat rate for a chunk of monthly use, from $15-$75 per month for 10-50 hours of online time, plus a small additional fee for time over that limit. My PPP service currently charges $25 a month for 25 hours of Net time, plus $1 per hour over those 25 hours; that's a good deal, without being the very best. Dialing these services is a local call in most cases.

Commercial online services charge a monthly fee (about $20 to $30) for a certain amount of use, an average of 40 hours per month. Some charge an hourly usage (anywhere from $2.95 to $10, depending on the time of day) for Internet access after a certain number of hours for a flat rate (between $8.95 and $20). Lately, many commercial services are wisely offering a certain amount of trial time accompanying new memberships—currently, new users of America Online, for example, receive ten hours to try out the service when they first subscribe. Don't forget to figure in long-distance tolls required to access any commercial service's dial-in number; if you live in a major city, you'll probably be able to access a local number.

I know of no commercial services that offer free *trial time; the new member must agree to subscribe first, and then cancel within the allotted trial time. I'm sure I'll hear if that changes.*

How much you spend for access depends on what you need: If you want jump-on-jump-off Internet access to simply read newsgroups and check your e-mail, I would seek an online service that offers reasonable hourly rates. If you don't care about e-mail and want to download massive amounts of data for your MIDI keyboard, you may be looking for raw Internet at the lowest possible bulk rate; I'd call your local Internet access providers and ask them for their SLIP/PPP connection rates. Get the most for your money, though, and don't be afraid to cancel your membership with one provider if your needs change.

How much software should you buy? If you use SLIP/PPP, you'll need WinSock and its supporting programs, all of which are available from the Internet itself. You'll also need your own Gopher, FTP, and Web-browsing applications if your Internet service provider doesn't supply them. Most of this additional software is readily available online, so don't buy anything unless you can't find it on the Net. If you join one of the commercial services, you'll need connecting software, which the company you've chosen will provide.

OTHER NECESSITIES

All the manuals and Read Me First files in the world can't teach you everything you need to know about the Internet, and that's part of what's cool about it. You'll learn some things by looking them up, but mostly you'll learn by doing—doing something wrong and screwing everything up for a moment; doing something right to your utter amazement; doing something so many times that you'll forget you didn't know how in the first place.

Like driving, doing work online requires knowledge of a few basic tools and terms. There are manners and language particular to the Net that, if you don't want to get *flamed* or *Bozo-filtered*, you'd be wise to learn.

Lingo

As do members of any organization, people on the Internet have a lingo all their own, an esoteric and often confusing language—until you know what they're talking about. In fact, Internetters revel in the fact that their lingo changes so fast: *WIRED* magazine's "Jargon Watch" column (see Figure 1.4) traces the monthly evolution of the newest and freshest words and phrases. As you may have already noticed, throughout this book I'll try to identify terms that might confuse you by putting them in *italics*—and following them with a definition that we can both understand.

Figure 1.4: WIRED magazine's "Jargon Watch" column digs up the newest of the new phrases and lingo.

A few basics will help; here's an alphabetical listing of some technical terms and some common Net lingo.

ASCII	a universal code for converting English letters and characters into binary code; also a method for copying files from one computer to another; pronounced "askey."
BBS	a bulletin board system; you already knew that.
Bozo-filtered	given the cold shoulder: In some chat rooms and e-mail programs, you can easily filter out someone whose comments you don't want to read.
BTW	By The Way...
chat rooms	places where you can type live messages back and forth with others online.

client	a computer seeking access to the services and information found on another computer, called a *server*.
download	move files or information from one computer to another, usually from a *server* to a *client*.
Gopher	one of the Internet's searching systems, an application the "goes-for" a subject you're looking for.
FAQ	Frequently Asked Questions, the answers to which are usually contained in a *FAQ File*.
flamed	chewed out by other online members for expressing something truly offensive or ignorant.
FTP	File Transfer Protocol, a way to transfer files back and forth between two computers.
FYI	For Your Information…
GIF	pronounced "jiff," one of several types of graphics file formats.
IP	Internet Protocol, one of the major connecting conventions used by two computers on the Net.
IRC	Internet Relay Channel, the live typing system used in the chat rooms.
JPEG	another graphics file format.
LOL	Laugh Out Loud, often preceded by *smileys*.
lurking	listening, watching, and observing in a newsgroup or chat room without making yourself known. You'll lurk first, then *post*.
MPEG	an animation file format that can include music, video, or graphics.
newbie	a new user, a Net tenderfoot with many stupid questions and misperceptions about what it's all about.
posts	messages written to other subscribers in a newsgroup. You "post to" a newsgroup or find one you want to "post in."
PPP	Point-to-Point Protocol, another connecting convention necessary between Internet computers.
ROFL or ROTFL	roll on (the) floor laughing, often preceded by *LOL*.
RTM	Read The Manual, often a suggestion worth heeding. Someone who tells you to *RTFM*, however, should learn some manners: He or she was once a newbie, too.

server	the remote computer that houses the info a *client* computer wants.
SLIP	like PPP, a necessary set of linking conventions between Net computers. SLIP and PPP are very similar.
site	a particular Internet location; on the WWW, sites are also called *pages*.
smileys	also called *emoticons*, little text-generated smiles, frowns, or winks (See "Smile—You're Online!") that you view by turning your head sideways.
TCP	like IP, Transfer Control Protocol is one of the major connecting conventions used by two computers on the Net.
TIFF	another graphics file format.
upload	move data from the server to the client.
URL	Uniform Resource Locator, the electronic address of a particular place on the Internet. FTP sites begin with ftp://; Web sites begin with http://.
WAIS	Wide Area Information Server, a searching tool like Gopher.
Web Browser	one of many programs supported on the World Wide Web, a simple application that lets you move between *URL*s very easily.

Smile—You're Online!

And, of course, there are smileys. Slightly too cute for their own good, *smileys*—also called *emoticons*—are those initially entertaining, but finally more annoying editorial comments that pepper Netspeech. You know the trick: Put your left ear on your left shoulder to see a digitized expression of someone

:)   smiling,

>l:-(frowning,

;)   winking, or

:-x   kissing/whose lips are sealed.

Net-addicts are forever trying tricky new things with their everyday keyboards, sending long-stemmed roses

@>—+—·+—·+—·

or

>>>>>hugs<<<<<

to each other. It's creative within the narrow bounds of the typewriter keys, so don't let it drive you

%-)   crazy.

Netiquette

Because the Net is growing (and has already grown) so big, manners are especially important. There aren't many rules for cruising the superhighway, but you've got to follow them.

First, when requesting any Internet services or online information, be as brief and polite as you can. Your brevity is crucial because, even though cyberspace seems infinite, your message still takes up room in a file somewhere; it's irresponsible to fill a screen with useless information just because you can.

Your politeness is necessary because human beings, not computers, eventually deal with many messages and, just as in any public forum, no one appreciates a rude or ill-mannered person. Your online anonymity gives you no right to be a demanding jerk.

Second, keep a roving eye on a clock while online. Colleges and universities are still the best sources for much Internet data, but schools need to serve their tuition-paying students first and foremost. Your middle-of-the-day FTP request that ties up one of their resources, when multiplied by millions of users world-wide, is potentially detrimental to thousands of students. So don't be selfish: Do your downloading or browsing at night or early in the morning; you'll have much better luck at accessing the info you want. Keep an atlas handy and memorize your time zones.

Third, remember what Mom taught you: Ignore the jerks and they'll go away. If someone is making a fool of himself online or inciting others around him, the best attitude is icy indifference. People who stir up hate on the Net are just itching for a reaction, and nothing pleases them more, in a chat room, for example, than to jump in and say something outrageous only to watch the sparks fly. Conversely, nothing shuts them up faster than cybersilence.

Ignore them. Bozo-filter them. Jump offline momentarily; they'll be gone soon. Don't waste the effort of typing a response to these cretins.

Gray Matter

What no book, not even this one, can teach is perhaps the best tool anyone can have, offline or online: Common sense. The Internet will do remarkable things for you, and take you to remarkable places, especially if you're seeking music. But you have to engage your brain.

In issues of security, for example, the anonymity of the Net contributes to both its safety and its risks: If you want to remain nameless for whatever reason, you can; if you want certain people to have certain information, you can supply it. Don't give anything to anyone without some credentials: Heavily guard information such as your full name, home address, telephone numbers, and passwords. You'll meet far more good-quality people on the Internet than jerks, but be wary of who has what information about you. Neutrality, credentials, caution, and safety are more than words; they're your guarantee to security and enjoyment on the Net.

The only sure indication of online credential seems to be longevity: The companies that successfully deal in business on the Internet—the service providers, software vendors, and (once you start seeking musical sites) the CD marketplaces and instrument swap-meets—have found a substantial new market. Like any marketers, it's in their best interests to provide top-quality products and reliable services, or they'll go out of business. My suggestion is to proceed with extreme caution, relying on recommendations and success-stories from your fellow Netizens.

 Beware, too, the evils of the credit card: Most business connections on the Internet are legitimate, but always—just as you do in real life—take steps to protect yourself by investigating services and purchases first. Protect those digits on your card at all costs, and ask around before you buy.

It may help to start thinking of the Internet as a community, one in which hundreds of thousands of people gather, doing whatever people do—working, playing, seeking others, seeking romance, making the most of their time, occasionally wasting it. As with any community, you'll encounter some Bozos and some frauds. But they'll make up the minority of humans you find in that community.

The Internet is first and foremost a place for communication, a medium for you to exercise your voice—and your typing skills. The Net is a place to speak your mind, to chat with old friends, to make new ones, to rant about something that makes you angry, to comfort someone who's out of sorts. The Internet is fiercely protective of that feeling of community, of the idea that everyone, each behind his or her computer terminal, is equal, that each single member should have access to all the information available out there in cyberspace, and that clear, direct, and meaningful communication is the most efficient way (maybe the *only* way) to achieve that access.

What Can You Do on the Net?

You've probably figured out by now that what the Internet *does* is at least as interesting as what it *is*.

Say you're a magazine editor who oversees your publication's music section: You may use the Net as a business resource, researching information for your writing, communicating with other writers who work for you, updating local calendar information. The Net provides you with a business tool that combines your voice-mail system, fact-checking department, and certain sections of your public library.

Or say you're a university student taking some singing classes, seeking a scholarship for grad school in addition to suggestions for improving your vocal techniques. The Net serves as an electronic medium that enhances your human endeavors, one that addresses both your current talent and the future of it.

I've designed this book for readers who want to utilize the Internet as a place to exploit their overlapping interest in music, computers, and the future of both. In this section you'll begin to glimpse the range of possibilities for what you can do on the Net, from the very first time you log on to a year from now when you're a Net-expert. You'll start simply, with e-mail, mailing lists, and newsgroups, and quickly become familiar with sophisticated processes like FTP downloading and the hypertext of the World Wide Web. Ready?

SOFTWARE 101.1: LEARNING TO GOPHER

The Internet is perhaps the single most remarkable information source in the world because it interconnects networks of data—from files of chili recipes to the most technical computer programs—and makes them available to the computer user. That mass of information, remarkable as it is, can be pretty intimidating when you're trying to find specific subject matter, such as recordings that feature both Duke Ellington and Count Basie together. Finding that proverbial needle in the haystack sounds pretty easy by comparison.

One thing that kept me away from computers for a long time is *techno-phobia*: When faced with a configuration diagram whose figures look like hieroglyphics, or requests for info or commands I've never heard of, I get worried. As a result, when I discover features or programs, such as Gopher, that think and act the way I do, I'm thrilled.

Gopher is an extremely efficient and user-friendly searching system that, along with a good computer, modem, and service provider, makes your exploitation of all the possibilities on the Internet very easy. Like the electromagnet that locates the needle, Gopher sleuths out remarkable things—the things you want. It's the perfect application to start with when tunneling into the first entries of this book.

Named for the Golden Gopher mascot at the University of Minnesota, where the little electronic mammal was born, Gopher is the information-finding software program designed to "go-for" info you're seeking on the Net. Gopher is a server connected to a system of servers that can, at the speed of light, collect valuable data for you from the Net.

Every Internet provider uses some form of information searching system, and Gopher is by far the most common. This system searches the archives using key words and phrases or titles and gives you back a list of what it's found that matches—more lists, files, documents, databases, and other network connections ranging from very specific topics (guitar chords to accompany "Stairway to Heaven") to very general ones for a specific subject (an archive directory of Gregorian chant files).

Gopher works with point-and-click simplicity: After you've logged on to the Net through your service provider, you open the Gopher software located on your hard disk (or, if you're using a commercial service that uses Gopher, on its host computer) to find various files available on the application's history and methodology as well as options to "Search All Gophers" or search any of a number of different Gopher sites.

That search section is where you want to be: Just enter the key phrases, terms, or subjects you want searched, request the search, and wait a bit. Gopher does the work and you get the data. A broad phrase like "alternative music" yields a long, very general list of FAQs and broadly-related files; a "Leonard Bernstein" search likewise gets you lots of files, with book titles, recordings, and related items. A search on the more esoteric topic "bagpipes" turns up just a few items—a couple of music files and some historical documents.

 Often, after searching, Gopher will announce it can find nothing under the key words you've requested, even if you've entered "Mick Jagger" or some other specific subject. All you need to do then is broaden (or narrow) your search parameters: Try "Rolling Stones" or "British pop music" or "Stones" (but be prepared, in that case, to get information on gem collecting as well). If your search continues to be fruitless, check alternative spellings.

One common problem, due to the fast growth of the Net, is recurring "lines busy" or "incomplete access" prompts. Remember that Gopher and other information-search systems are heavily used, often much more so than their design allows. If you're searching for something and your Gopher keeps coming up empty-pawed, either try another Gopher site (if that's an option) or try at another time of day, even a few minutes later. Remember that cyberspace is a busy place.

 It's important to note the variety of types of documents you receive from your completed Gopher search. Some are simple text files, which you can open immediately with the next click or command. Some are files of more information, which may include text, under a broader heading.

Often you'll open up something that's just a list of slashes and lines and cryptic abbreviations: What good does http://www.iuma.com/ do me, anyway, if I requested info on the band American Music Club?

Well, that hostile-looking http://www.iuma.com/ is called a *URL*—Uniform Resource Locator, a location-specific Internet address for (in this case) one of the best musical archive sites on the World Wide Web (see "Internet Underground Music Archive" in the "Alternative Music" section of Part Two). From this site you can download a beautiful digitally rendered copy of American Music Club's most current cover art and audio samples of their songs. So keep that URL handy.

Like so many skills on the Net, requesting, searching, interpreting, and downloading information that Gopher and other searching systems provide takes practice and patience. What's great about Gopher, however, is that you can master its techniques very quickly and get on to the more important stuff it's unearthed for you.

FUNDAMENTALS: E-MAIL AND MAILING LISTS

From Bach to the Beastie Boys, music is one of civilization's oldest ways to communicate, and pairing music with this remarkable form of communication—the Internet—only makes sense. As a community, the Internet is a place where all voices are equal, where the most fundamental activity is that of one-to-one communication. Electronic mail is the easiest way to begin communicating on the Net.

E-mail is a streamlined way to send (and receive) personal messages. When you sign up with a service provider, you're assigned a particular slice of cyberspace all your own, just like a post office box: It stores messages until you decide to read them; it opens and closes at your command.

Because e-mail is a basic Internet service, this book doesn't include a particular section on e-mail as it relates to music. Many musicians do maintain e-mail addresses (you can, for example, send e-mail to Billy Idol by addressing to idol@phantom.com, *if you're so inclined), but I would suggest treating pop stars' e-mail addresses like fan club addresses, anticipating that you may or may not get a personal reply from your favorite artists.*

INTRODUCTION TO MAILING LISTS

My *snail mail*—regular old-fashioned mail—gets delivered late in the afternoon, and I eagerly paw through the stack, hoping to find something interesting or personal among the bills, junk mail, and magazine offers. Yet three-fourths of what I receive goes right into the recycling bucket. It seems as if personal mail—relevant and meaningful documents delivered directly to you at your home or business—has vanished, replaced by low-rate and direct-market advertising.

But imagine a mailbox that fills daily with pertinent information from colleagues, friends, and specifically chosen organizations from whom you've requested information. The "mailbox," of course, is your e-mail address, where you'll receive everything from co-workers' wedding announcements to up-to-the-minute information from your Internet service provider. Unlike snail mail, e-mail provides (with a little tailoring on your part) mail that reflects your interests and needs rather than a barrage of useless junk.

One of the most fundamental (and enjoyable) uses for your e-mail system, besides communicating with individuals, is subscribing to *mailing lists*. Mailing lists work exactly like pieces of e-mail, except that instead of receiving

E-mail Addresses: Not as Confusing as They Seem

Internet addresses identify a particular Internet source using categories of increasing generality. The *domains*—the group of network hosts, similar to the parts of a mailing address, that make it a unique Internet stop—give you clues to the sources of information. Let's dissect an e-mail address:

sfisk@alm.admin.usfca.edu

Reading left to right, this address indicates someone whose username is sfisk, working @ (the "at" symbol, used only in e-mail addresses) a host computer called alm located in the admin (probably "administration") section of usfca (in this case, the "University of San Francisco, California"), an edu ("educational") institution. This last domain, called a *top-level domain*, can be one of several types of organizations: Here are some others:

com	Commercial	mil	U.S. Military
gov	U.S. Government	net	Networks and Information Centers
org	Nonprofit		

personal messages from individuals, you receive them from a group of people who share similar interests—for music aficionados, these can include fan clubs, record companies, musical organizations, or devotees of a particular genre or instrument. A mailing list is just like a newsletter: as one of its subscribers, every so often—once a week, once a month, every few days, it depends on the list's preference—you'll receive an updated batch of compiled information on its subject.

Mailing lists revive your interest in getting mail; they make going to the mailbox—Click! Click!—worth the trip. This book, while not an exhaustive roster, offers a broad reference to available musical mailing lists. Use *A Pocket Tour of Music on the Internet* as a jumping-off place to get to your first stops, and then get ready for frequent flying.

SUBSCRIBING TO A MAILING LIST

Subscribing to mailing lists is the simplest form of exploring music on the Internet. You need only the tools you have to send regular e-mail: Your computer, a connection to the Internet (and/or the working modem to get you online), and a mail program with a working e-mail address. But before you go any further, just make sure you have the following:

◆   the software installed to run your modem (if you're running SLIP/PPP) and an e-mail program on the Net

◆   an Internet provider that has e-mail capabilities (all commercial services and most providers do)

What's the best mailing list to start with? One suggestion is to choose a fan club you're interested in for your first subscription: From your *Pocket Tour of Music on the Internet*, pick something you'd be interested to read for a month or so. Then simply open the program on your Internet e-mail software to a blank mail page or template, return to your book, and follow the directions that follow the title of the listing, like this:

1.   In the address section of a blank mail document, type the "To sub-scribe" address, probably something like LISTSERV@ucsd.edu.

2.   If the directions ask for your full name or your e-mail address, give them *exactly*. If they ask you to place a command in the body of the letter, do so.

3.   If your mail template requires a "Subject" line, just fill it in simply; if the list request form hasn't asked for any subject, the computer answering the request won't read it.

4.   If something seems askew because the directions don't ask for your e-mail address, remember that your address automatically appears on everything you send out; the computer mailing program will read it automatically.

Don't make any stray marks in the template—no extra periods, dashes, or spaces between characters—because any deviation from the listed address could cause trouble in cyberspace.

While some lists also have a single address for everything, most require the new subscriber to send requests for services to a *list manager*—the comput-er that receives requests for subscribing and unsubscribing—not to the list itself. You send *articles*—submissions you've written—to the articles address, and requests for service to "LISTSERV" or "Majordomo" addresses, where you'll find the *list manager*.

Think of it like this: If you wanted to start receiving Channel 22 on your cable TV, you wouldn't call Channel 22 itself, you'd call your cable company.

You'll often notice references to sending a "politely-worded request" instead of a command. It's always a good idea to err on the side of politeness when communicating online. Although it's a computer-based communication mode, the Net runs on human organization. Be friendly; be patient. If a computer is screwing up, a human will eventually have to fix things, and he or she prefers polite interaction. Likewise, consider how many excellent resources on the Net are free: The least you can do is say please and thank you. Thanks for listening.

Save that first piece of e-mail you receive from the list (often a simple confirmation message) because it usually contains info on getting help, unsubscribing, receiving rosters of members, and other particular list services. If you decide you want off a list, just follow its instructions for unsubscribing (or follow instructions from the entries in this book).

It's rude to subscribe and immediately unsubscribe to a mailing list. Because lists are run voluntarily, someone somewhere has to do extra work because you were too lazy to figure out that the MORRIS list was about dancing and

House Coffee? Cappuccino? Internet?

Imagine a huge coffee shop or café where only music buffs hang out, dozens of groups talking in passionate depth about certain musical subjects. Several conversations are going on simultaneously within each group, and everyone is able to follow every conversation. Sound cool? One of the most simple, rewarding tasks to do on the Internet, joining a newsgroup is exactly like entering that coffee shop.

Subscribing to Net newsgroups allows you to receive pertinent advice or guidance from qualified experts on a subject you'd like to know more about, to hang with colleagues, to discuss in detail a subject you all know well. Newsgroups, some of the few Net-places that are always friendly, are those corners in cyberspace where everyone has voluntarily agreed to pursue one particular subject, where nothing else—or, rather, *everything pertinent*—is discussed. It's where Enya fans can post about Enya until they're blue in the monitor.

Using your Internet service provider for

not about cats. So do your research before you request a subscription, and—for now—stick with the lists you've chosen.

If you send a subscription request and it comes right back (usually from what's called a *mailer daemon*) indicating an unknown address, double-check the request and try again: have you spelled everything right? If you continue to have trouble, do a Gopher search by title for another address in the same category. If that doesn't work, try a different category, broadening or narrowing your parameters with each successive search. Before long, you'll be collecting interesting reading from your virtual mailbox, printing the text of your first mailing list, and enjoying it with the next morning's coffee.

 Certain commercial services still charge customers by the piece for e-mail they receive, a ridiculous practice if you ask me. If you're affected by such charges, remember that some mailing lists regularly send out new versions.

BREAKING THE ICE: JOINING NEWSGROUPS

Joining a newsgroup takes your mailing list skills one step further. Newsgroups feature ongoing discussions between interested parties on particular subjects, including a variety of musical topics, from Slint to Stone Temple Pilots to Stravinsky. Joining and reading newsgroups is similar to reading your e-mail: Just use the particular method your service requires—

access, you can choose your newsgroups in several ways:

- Browse the lists of groups to whom your service provides access (which, in most cases, will include all the groups in this book).

- Search by group name for those you're interested in (although these supposedly helpful systems have a few glitches, which you'll hear about shortly).

- Search more effectively by subject.

- Most easily, scan your *Pocket Tour* for a comprehensive list of fan groups, special interest groups, music makers' groups, and a broad mix of genre styles.

So c'mon in: no matter what you're drinking (Double espresso? De-caf mocha?) or listening to (Shellac? Sir Mix-A-Lot? Coltrane?), there's an open seat at the musical newsgroup of your choice.

pointing and clicking, entering a keyword (which some commercial services use to quickly jump you from place to place), or selecting from menu items. You have the opportunity to add or delete newsgroups, to search for ones you're interested in by subject or title, and to read the ones in which you've chosen to participate.

As you do with mailing lists, you choose the newsgroups where you want to observe, and eventually, post. You don't have to contribute if you don't want to; there are more lurkers than posters in any given newsgroup. You will want to post to one, though, sooner or later.

Some groups are run by people much younger than you, some much older; some groups seem hostile, some warm and welcoming. Some attract members who spell poorly; some attract loudmouths or self-righteous jerks. But most newsgroups are exactly what you'd hope: Forums where everyone's equal and each has a voice. It's simply a matter of finding the groups, electing to join them, reading their posts, and deciding if they'll sustain your interest.

You may discover some frustrations when investigating newsgroups: Some forums exist but have no postings; others strangely duplicate themselves with different titles; occasionally you'll hear about a perfect one, but no amount of perseverance can get you connected with it.

Some musical newsgroups are predictable, their popularity matching that of their subject: There are the requisite rec.music.beatles and alt.fan.madonna and alt.fan.elvis-presley. But there are also unexpected stops like rec.music.makers.guitar. tabulature, where you can find guitar chords in text files to accompany your favorite songs, or alt.music.filk, a group dedicated to a strange and unclassifiable space where music and science fiction overlap. Some forums are hard to classify, such as the rec.music.classical.guitar, a place for fans of the genre and working musicians alike.

As you begin to seek out musical mailing lists and newsgroups, you'll find that Gopher's efficient subject-searching and locating abilities will expand your access. Keep in mind that working on the Internet requires a balance of software efficiency, hardware capability, and human creativity. As you move into more sophisticated Internet processes and accompanying applications, you'll learn even more—and the payoffs will be even greater.

Compuserve calls its newsgroups forums. *Some people use the terms* newsgroup *and* forum *interchangeably.*

SUBSCRIBING TO NEWSGROUPS

I propose two ways to jump into the world of newsgroups: The first is to track down rec.music.info, a forum with constantly changing, remarkably complete Internet sources related to music. Besides charts and concert dates, rec.music.info has FAQ files, addresses, and FTP and WWW locations indispensable for every Net user.

Another effective way is to pursue one or more groups found in Part Two. The Author's Pick icons point you toward the most interesting sites.

To subscribe to a group, make sure:

◆ you have a service provider that supports newsgroups (most providers and all commercial services do)

◆ you have correctly entered the address of the group you want to access, either by name or subject, in your service's "searching" or "adding" sections

◆ the group still exists

Each Internet service provider has a different method for adding newsgroups, but it's usually as simple as jumping online, entering the Newsgroup or Usenet area of your service provider, and searching for the group you want to explore. Your point-and-click method will vary with the service you've chosen, but once you're either searching or adding, you're moments away from reading posts, marveling at the variety of listings and the personalities behind them, and carefully wording your first response.

With thousands of newsgroups on the Net, providers cannot possibly link to all of them. If you discover a newsgroup you want to join that you can't access, contact your system administrator.

The only law of newsgroupland is that posts be pertinent, brief (some are ridiculously so), and timely. Many forums are moderated—edited for content before posts appear—but if censorship is a problem, a particular newsgroup can always splinter into another. Learning how to add newsgroups will pay off in the first fifteen minutes you spend skimming files, noting addresses, and observing conversation in your new café.

If you get the urge to start your own group, begin by posting an *RFD*—a Request For Discussion—in news.announce.newgroups, and then pass through the prescribed channels before your forum becomes published. See the section "news.announce.newgroups" in the "Folk and Country Music" section of Part Two to learn how to do that.

If you don't immediately find the group you're looking for, don't be disappointed: You probably just haven't defined it the same way a computer does. If you want to join a mainstream newsgroup you're sure exists, just persevere in your search for it, using your instincts. Maybe what seems like evasiveness is just obscurity, or maybe the group hasn't yet been formed, and you should think about creating it.

Once you've chosen groups you want to test out, joining them is simple. Depending on your service provider, you can simply add them as stops to your newsgroup list, and the next time you elect to read your news, they'll be there waiting for you.

*Newsgroups tend to be either narrowly focused fan groups or very broad subject groups, yet something in between is optimal. The best group for me is one that focuses on a particular style of music (*alt.exotic-music *and* rec.music. afro-latin *come to mind) but leaves its discussion wide open within those subject parameters.*

Notice the tiny difference between the-doors *and* the.police*: When searching for newsgroup information, be exact in your addressing: The difference between a hyphen and a period (or* dot*) may not seem like an important detail, but your searching system may drive you crazy if it's unable to differentiate.*

Remember that no searching system is infallible. Although a computer is infinitely patient (as it tells you for the umpteenth time that the subject you're asking for is too broad), remember that the old cliché is wrong—a computer is *not* as smart as the person running it, it's just more stubborn.

SOFTWARE 101.2: LEARNING FTP AND OTHER DOWNLOADING METHODS

After you become comfortable subscribing to mailing lists and reading newsgroups, you'll find yourself wanting to delve into the Internet's remarkable archives. You'll develop an appetite for the Internet's *FTP sites*—places accessible on the Internet from which you can download text files, graphics files, sound and video files, and software programs to enhance your musical expertise.

FTP: Your Online Librarian

A s a graduate student a few years ago, I met a remarkable librarian, a tiny woman who worked in the reference section of my university library.

Supplied with just a title or author's name, she could ferret out and pluck from the shelves an obscure book—exactly *the* obscure book—I needed for particular research I was doing. Hemingway to Ibsen to composition theory, it didn't matter the subject: she would scratch her head, look skyward, and shuffle directly to where the book I needed lay, saving me cumulative hours of searching.

Think of FTP as a very efficient librarian in a massive research library: You ask the program to retrieve a certain file for you, feeding your computer exact information, including where the machine that contains the data is located, what password is needed to access it, and what directory holds the file you want to access.

Supplied with this information, FTP zooms to its task, jumping through those sequential hoops until it locates the data. A final word from you, and FTP downloads it—sluuur-rrp!—onto your computer. Slick. FTP is the system that places copies of files gathered from a *server* (a remote computer) onto a *client* (another computer, probably yours).

Very well, you say, but what if I don't know exactly which FTP site I'm looking for? Just as Gopher is an extremely efficient subject-searching application, user-friendly *Archie* searches for FTP sites by filename. You can find copies of Archie in software libraries or elsewhere for the taking.

In this ever-expanding informational day and age, a good librarian—and FTP—is good to know.

FTP, as I mentioned earlier, is used as a noun, verb, and adjective: FTP (File Transfer Protocol) is the system by which one computer (probably yours) downloads information from another (probably one overflowing with musical information). When you look for such a file, you're seeking one "available for FTP;" when you eventually download it, you could say you "FTPed" the file. Also, once you find it or download it, you may well recognize it as an "FTP file" you got from an "FTP site."

Should an English major write a computer book?

FTP requires a little more Net expertise to operate than does Gopher, and requires more detailed information from the user to do its work—more, say, than a simple subject or an e-mail address. Because of the nature and sophistication of its job, an FTP application is also more likely to go wrong; occasionally it won't go at all.

But the payoff is that when it does, its services are remarkably rewarding. If you're like me—someone who for years used his computer as a glorified word processor—you'll get a thrill when you successfully load a piece of software, a GIF of your favorite artist, or a snippet of recorded music onto your very own machine and view or play it back for the first time.

The first thing to download when you learn FTP is the most current version of a disinfectant application for your hard disk. Because you'll be accessing files from all over the world, protecting your system from potential viruses should be your first priority. Find one at: ftp://ftp.acns.nwu.edu/pub/disinfectant.

What about *anonymous FTP*? When I first began learning about downloading, the term sounded sinister and covert, as though I were sneaking in somewhere I shouldn't be to retrieve something I had no business seeing. Anonymous FTP, however, is nothing more than a system that makes files publicly available. When using anonymous FTP, you log in to the remote machine with the username "anonymous."

In some cases an FTP server will, for reasons of security, require that you enter a password; some won't. If an FTP site asks for a password, there's a reason for it; if you feel positive you should be accessing that machine but don't know a password, supply the terms "anonymous" or "newuser" at the *login* prompt, and then, for your password, use your e-mail address.

I first learned to FTP on one of the commercial services, where *userids*— that's "user IDs" to you and me—and passwords are all but eliminated (see Figure 1.5). This system may be the wave of the future: More and more, FTP software lets you get places without the encumbering passwords.

Some documents you download may require you to decompress them or convert them from one file type to another. Applications that do all these conversions—the racy sounding *unzipping* and *unstuffing*, which simply

Figure 1.5:
CompuServe's Anonymous FTP program is very simple to use.

unfold a document from its traveling size to its viewing size—are available if you know where to look: Try the software libraries of your service provider or snoop around the same FTP site you're using. It's not a big problem, but it will come up from time to time.

Downloader's law: You won't figure out that a file needs to be converted until you're long gone from the FTP site. Get in the habit of checking your documents while you're still there.

FTP, like any Internet activity, requires some etiquette. Anytime you're using it, do your business, check your file, and head back home; don't crowd FTP sites during daylight hours if you can help it. As Net traffic increases, you'll probably see more and more mirror sites; when at all possible, use the one geographically closest to you.

DOWNLOADING FILES

Your first step for successfully downloading files via FTP is deciphering a URL into its domains. A variation on e-mail addresses, URLs are divided into parts that read in *increased* specificity from left to right. Here's an example:

ftp://sounds.sdsu.edu/sounds/usr/demo/SOUND/play

This URL indicates an ftp source located (this much is like an e-mail address) on the sounds machine located at sdsu ("San Diego State University"), an educational organization. Then things get more complex: Nested in the sounds directory are increasingly specific directories or files—the demo inside the usr, the SOUND inside the demo, and so on—and eventually, a particular file (play), publicly available for you to download.

Once you decipher the URL, the rest is easy. After you've arrived online, you simply:

1. Start up your FTP program.

2. Enter the information between the paired slashes (//) and the first single slash—in this case, sounds.sdsu.edu—in FTP's site-specific search section.

3. Ask FTP to connect you to that host.

URLs are like targets (see Figure 1.6) or maps: Just as you use an address to locate a snail-mailing address in a particular country, state, and city, you use a URL to locate, in this case, a file related to music. Simple.

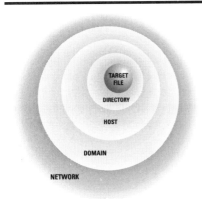

Figure 1.6:
Think of a URL as a series of concentric circles, with the file you want at the center of the target.

Once you're connected to the site itself, you begin by opening the largest directory (sounds), and then look for usr, demo, and so forth.

Many programs have a system of bookmarks—*favorite sites you can type out once and save in a list; those commercial services with FTP capability offer a list of suggested sites as well.*

There is a world of difference between how a PC user running a command-line interface retrieves files using FTP and how a point-and-click user does it.

I'll start with the easy group: If you have a software program that transfers files using a point-and-click interface, you search files exactly as you open them on your machine: By clicking (or double-clicking) on icons, getting more specific until you reach the file you want to use (see Figure 1.7). Using our example above, you would very quickly reach the desired play file, and then click on "Download" (or whatever word your program uses) to transfer the file onto your machine. If this method describes you, you're finished with the FTP section of this book, and I'll meet you by the pool.

If you're using Unix commands to navigate the Internet, the first thing you'll see after connecting to the remote computer via FTP (and you may need

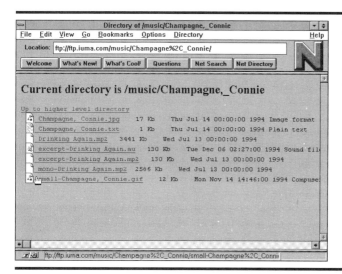

Figure 1.7:
When using a graphic interface, you open nested FTP files just as you do regular files on your computer.

to enter your "anonymous" username and your e-mail address password) is an ftp> prompt. From here you simply issue the commands for the particular file you need. If you're stuck, use "Unix, Schumix" as an easy reference.

You'll usually know whether you're seeking text files (of written information) or binary files (graphics, audio, or video), but make sure the files you're downloading are in the correct format.

Your FTP program will provide a simple screen to guide you through the downloading process (see Figure 1.8). It's far easier to FTP than I can explain in these few pages: Take my word for it. As programs and interfaces become easier

Figure 1.8:
The screen FTP you'll see if you're running Windows 95. Others may look very similar.

to use, an initially intimidating process like FTP is not much more complicated than sending e-mail, subscribing to a mailing list, or joining a newsgroup.

SOFTWARE 101.3: LEARNING TO USE WEB BROWSERS

Born in the early 1990s as a medium for European physicists to share interrelated files and documents, the World Wide Web has quickly outgrown its original intent. Besides being one of cyberspace's most exciting places, the World Wide Web (also called, you remember, the *Web* or *WWW*) is the best example to date of the possibilities for Net technology.

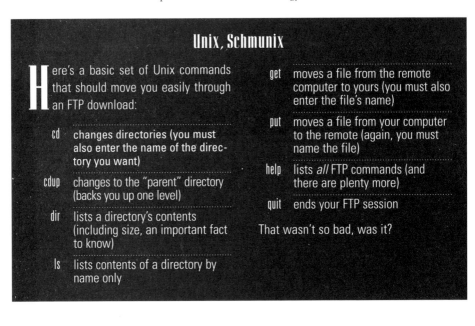

Unix, Schmunix

Here's a basic set of Unix commands that should move you easily through an FTP download:

cd   changes directories (you must also enter the name of the directory you want)

cdup   changes to the "parent" directory (backs you up one level)

dir   lists a directory's contents (including size, an important fact to know)

ls   lists contents of a directory by name only

get   moves a file from the remote computer to yours (you must also enter the file's name)

put   moves a file from your computer to the remote (again, you must name the file)

help   lists *all* FTP commands (and there are plenty more)

quit   ends your FTP session

That wasn't so bad, was it?

The WWW is a multilevel encyclopedia of text, graphic files, audio files, and video files, all brought to life on a user-friendly interface built of logical commands and simple instructions. It's a place to simply browse, "crawling" from *Website* to *Website* (or, as they say, from *page* to *page*), or a place where you can conduct research, all with the click of a button. It's also a valuable source for locating other Internet resources—FTP and Gopher sites, newsgroups, and many others. Most importantly, the Web, unlike many other Internet systems, is immediately useable by any Net surfer, from the tinkering novice to the savvy expert.

With the invention of the Web browser program known as Mosaic, the National Center for Supercomputing Applications (NCSA) at the University of Illinois, Urbana/Champaign, has created a remarkable program that utilizes *hypertext*—a nonlinear method of transmitting and reading data. Now a standard application for *Web browsers*—programs that traverse the Web— Mosaic utilizes hypertext in a way that denizens of the Net can not only understand, but can comfortably exploit almost immediately.

Several forms of Mosaic are commercially available, all of which are enhanced forms of NCSA Mosaic, the original. For a complete reference to all the Mosaics and Netscape, a very popular Mosaic-type Net browser (see Figure 1.9), check out Sybex's Mosaic Roadmap, ©1995.

WORLD WIDE WEB DOCUMENTS

Consider the simple act of reading a page of text: If English is your native language, you probably do so from left to right, and—most likely—from top to bottom. You could read from bottom to top, of course, and even from right to left, getting a particular slant (and perhaps a headache) from doing so.

But what if you could read beneath the surface of that text, or above it? What if particular terms within the text itself—a proper name, a geographical reference, or some other detail—could be read in *depth*, either to gain a different perspective, an overview, or a detailed focus of the subject at hand?

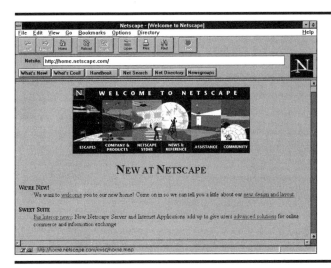

Figure 1.9:
Netscape's Welcome screen is one you'll probably become very familiar with.

A Quick Spin around the Web

L et's put this hyperactivity in context. Say I'm interested in the underground music scene: From a friend, I happen to get the URL for a new online magazine on the Web. I jack in, have a look around. One of its articles is on college radio, with hotlinks to several stations around the country.

I link to a station located in a city I'm going to be visiting in a couple of weeks. I read about its types of programming, and then discover a calendar section discussing upcoming events the station is promoting. One such event is a local music festival underwritten by a local nonprofit group that also maintains a Web page.

I click in to their page, reading more about the group and the festival, browsing the roster of bands that are playing. The line-up looks great to me: I see one of my favorite bands is slated at a nightclub that has its own URL. I'm there in a flash.

The club's page gives me ticket prices and directions to the venue, and mentions some other benefits the club has done, one for an independent record company I've heard of but would like to know more about.

I click on the record company's hotlink, and in no time I'm skimming back-catalogues, reading biographies, and downloading a price list. Several of their artists maintain fan clubs on the Web, so I begin to check those out one by one, watching videos, perhaps hearing audio clips from upcoming releases. . . .

See how it works? Incorporating a half-dozen sites, that combination is but one possibility among millions.

Wouldn't it be great to read a page of text that anticipates your need for additional information?

Hypertext does just that: When you're using Mosaic or any other browser, certain words, phrases, or icons are highlighted to indicate that more information about them lies beneath the page. Clicking on these highlighted items—Mosaic calls them *hotlinks*—connects you to another page that gives supporting details, overviews, and additional related resources available on that subject. Using hypertext is like reading in three dimensions.

 In print, this sounds a little like trying to leap onto a whirling carousel, so I should make it clear: As you sign on to the WWW, you're automatically delivered to a home page—a Website that is your starting place. Every Web browser has a home page.

From the home page, you begin your exploration, whether by using hotlinks or by defaulting to another Web page whose URL you type in. It's safe and easy, and you can backtrack (or return home) at any point by clicking the navigating buttons.

Web-crawling couldn't be any easier. After arriving online, you simply:

1. Start up Mosaic (or whatever browser you've chosen), which delivers you to its defaulted home page.

2. Enter the URL you want in the URL box (making sure to type it exactly), and press ↵.

3. Begin your crawl by using hotlinks, the directional buttons, or by entering another URL.

That's all there is to it. The WWW is your final payoff, the best and last stop on this tour. See you in a few pleasurable hours.

Some browsers have built-in searching systems that allow you to investigate by subject if you wish. Most often, however, you'll start with a known URL: They seem to be proliferating like telephone numbers.

Whether you're taking your first tenuous steps on the Internet or surfing and spinning with ease, you can easily access the remarkable cross-section of resources—from simple mailing lists to in-depth newsgroups, from the ripe FTP sites to the stunningly beautiful graphics glistening on a Web page—from that machine at your desk. For the computer user who likes his music or the music buff who tinkers with her computer, this book is your guide to this community where people just like you are enjoying the music that plays and plays.

And if you're like me, you're restless to get started.

What follows in your *Pocket Tour of Music on the Internet* are the hundreds of entries where you'll find all the resources we've been talking about: Mailing lists, Newsgroups, FTP sites, and Websites. With the expertise you've accumulated in these first pages, tracking down the sites you find in the following pages will be a breeze. You're moments away from enjoying the very subject that led you to pick up this book in the first place—music on the Internet.

Off we go....

Part Two:
The Sites

Alternative Music

An alternative medium itself, the Internet has always been the logical place to expose "alternative" music. This first section of Part Two pays homage to those genres, musicians, and record companies that truly resist categorization, those cutting-edge Internet resources reaping the benefits of this remarkable new multimedium.

Though many commercial radio stations may describe their programming as "alternative," they still appeal to a mainstream audience. In this section, I use the word *alternative* to describe music that differs from the mainstream, music that draws a fair-sized audience but clearly defines itself as being not for everyone. If you're seeking big-name "alternative" acts, check the listings in "Rock and Pop."

If you're a newbie scanning this section for the first time, it may appear to you that the Internet is a twentysomething clique, overflowing with obscure musical topics and artists. That's not true: The Internet features music of *all* kinds, and, like newspapers, radio, or television, is fast becoming a medium for the general public; you only need to know where to look.

ALTERNATIVE MUSIC: GENERAL LISTINGS

If you're seeking starting places in this section, you might try the alt.music. alternative *or* rec.music.info *newsgroups: Both are large and general enough to offer something for everyone.*

Alternative Music

alt.music.alternative

With thousands of postings accumulating monthly, alt.music.alternative's subject matter is hard to define. It leans, however, toward next week's commercial-alternative radio favorites: Heavy on Liz Phair, Ween, Soundgarden, Veruca Salt, and the Cranberries—*this* month. This site seems to be one of the largest alternative musical newsgroups, and a good starting place to prove the sheer variety of forums available to you. Stop by with plenty of time on your hands and I guarantee you'll find someone who'll trade posts with you.

Canadian Alternative Music

alt.music.canada

alt.music.canada's best feauture was also its most frustrating for me: The fact that it focuses, as promised, on the Canadian alternative scene. Because of the site's specificity, I had heard of few of the discussed artists. You'll find frequent references to MuchMusic (the Canadian MTV), tons of Canadian band listings, and space devoted to working musicians (studios for rent, bands looking for members) with a focus on the western provinces and Pacific Northwest. Although I didn't find much to satisfy my own interests, alt.music.canada seemed to have a small but growing group of devotees.

Newsgroup Glossary

Here are a few helpful terms to know when checking out your first newsgroup:

administrator also called the *system administrator*, the person or people who decide which newsgroups your particular network can access. Most networks can access most newsgroups.

flame you remember this one: to lash out at someone, using just a keyboard with the CAPS LOCK key on.

forum a term some people use interchangeably with *newsgroup*.

moderator the person who reads all submitted posts and decides which to include. Not all newsgroups have moderators.

post to write a message for the group's audience; also the message itself.

thread a discussion topic that members *post* about until a more interesting thread comes along. Usually several are going at once.

Category Freaks

alt.music.category-freak

An unfortunate trend in music these days is the need to categorize it all: This is grunge, this is acid jazz, this is rap. But some music pops from any box in which you try to stuff it. For that reason, alt.music.category-freak exists: If you can't quite put your finger on your favorite artist's genre, you may find that artist here. Minimalist composer Terry Riley, The Velvet Underground (which incubated American songwriting geniuses Lou Reed, Moe Tucker, and John Cale), and unclassifiable jazzman Fred Frith had listings on a recent visit. If your taste in music means you have a hard time locating it in a music store, try this group. It's a good directory for general information that may point you toward other sites—FTP archives, WWW pages, or specific newsgroups or mailing lists—that feature more obscure artists.

Some networks cannot access alt.music.category-freak; *if you're connected to one, contact your system administrator and ask him or her to add this excellent newsgroup.*

Cyberdog Music Database

http://www.magicnet.net/rz/three_minute_dog/cyberdog.html

An organization that uses technology to help out up-and-coming musicians, Cyberdog began as Three Minute Dog, a group of music industry professionals dedicated to establishing touring routes, promotion, and demo production for "artists taking control of their own career development." Cyberdog's database links you to U.S. college radio sites, including many community- and university-funded stations (see Figure 2.1). Elsewhere on the site, you'll find tutorials that explain how to promote your own band and provide other important industry tips. A must-stop for the new artist with an eye on the future.

Though it's still in the works, Cyberdog is also making plans for a database that would link independent- and major-label record distributors, for use by promoters, fans, and working artists who want to get their material distributed.

Figure 2.1 :
Radio station KFJC's logo. KFJC is one of many college stations in all fifty states linked to the Cyberdog site.

KFJC 89.7FM Foothill College Radio Info
Cool Taste in Heavy Sounds

Eden Matrix Archive

http://www.eden.com/eden/eden.html

The self-described Austin, Texas "underground infobahn" is closely affiliated with the concert industry's *Pollstar* magazine. This site houses videos and audio demos for an excellent cross-section of signed and unsigned bands. Downloads are free. Check out their occasional Internet broadcasts (they'll set you up with the software you need) and their still-under-construction Austin club directory. This site also houses the Dejadisc and Mesa record companies.

Electronic Body and Industrial Music

alt.music.ebm

The informative FAQ from this European-run newsgroup says it best: "EBM...is an acronym for 'Electronic Body Music,' a general splinter group of 'industrial' music. Labels that have been used to describe this group include: Electro/Electrobeat (noisy rhythmic sounds), Cold Wave (southern CA derivative), Industrial Dance (generic term), Techno (as defined in a German context), Aggreppo (merging of aggressive and pop), Aggro (aggressive electronics), Technocore and Cyberpunk." Got that? If you were born to dance all night and can differentiate between Zoth Onmog and RAS DVA, you'll appreciate the discussions, discographies, and club events that ebm has to offer.

Electronic Music

alt.emusic

Just what is a pitch-MIDI converter, anyway? This newsgroup for electronic musicians is heavy on the gear—Lyricons, Roland 1080s, new and used Prophets—so if it's emusic paraphernalia you're seeking, whether you're the leader of Tangerine Dream or just a basement tinkerer, this is your niche. Someone's looking for analog synthesizers, someone else for patches or library systems for their sampler. A dozen or so FTP sites list the latest keyboard software programs.

Fanbases include Depeche Mode—mercifully few—to Frente! and Martin Denny. Do these people ever leave their homes? Sure: L.A.'s "ambient club," the Nocturne Lounge, has a listing for upcoming events. A little emusic humor, tucked inside instructions for a complicated patchwork configuration: "Smash forehead on keyboard to continue." I guess you have to be there....

Exotic Music

alt.exotic-music

Everything old is new again: Partly because of *RE/Search* magazine's *Incredibly Stange Music* CD series, retro-chic exotica is all the rage lately, with artists like Combustible Edison and Love Jones donning cummerbunds and ruffled shirts and dishing out swanky lounge Muzak while the audience sips hi-balls under tiki torchlight. alt.exotic-music, while hip to that scene, seems to suffer a little from postings about music that someone decided was exotic just because it isn't mainstream: Chinese contemporary songwriters, Italian composer Nono Rota, and Les Negresses Vertes may be exotic, but they're removed from the *fabulous*ness that marks true exotica artists like Juan Garcia Esquivel and Ken Baxter. If hip swing is your thing, keep a roving eye on alt.exotic-music, which, as it gains focus, will probably define a whole new class—in the sense of classy—of Netiquette.

General Musical Information

rec.music.info

So you want to subscribe to the Sugar mailing list, start your own university-based musical newsgroup, and eventually download from your favorite artists' World Wide Web page? Not geared specifically toward alternative tastes, but rather toward *all* music, rec.music.info is a good starting place for your newsgroup interest. Straightforward and easy to use, it features charts, mailing lists, info, concerts, discographies, releases, and FAQs for your every musical need—a directory of sorts to the other newsgroups. It's exhaustively complete, although incredibly random; it can answer most preliminary questions about any newsgroup you want to join, as well as provide info on how to start your own.

Generation X

X

Can't really say what the "Generation-X lifestyle" is, but the mailing list, for those interested in the phenomenon, defines its subscribers as "being young or young at heart, listening to strange music that makes older people queasy, and generally having no set purpose or direction in life." If this is a portrait of you, subscribe today. Or, don't. You know, whatever.

Owner or Contact Ken Pierce, KPierce@age.cuc.ab.ca

To Subscribe E-mail LISTSERV@age.cuc.ab.ca; in the body of the message, type **SUBSCRIBE** *your e-mail address X*. To unsubscribe, send the command **UNSUB X** in e-mail to LISTSERV@age.cuc.ab.ca. Send all other list-related commands to LISTSERV@age.cuc.ab.ca. For assistance, send the command **HELP**. Send all articles to X@age.cuc.ab.ca.

Grindcore/Death Metal/Heavy Thrash Music

GRIND

Trust me: If you're a fan of grindcore, you *know* it. Faster than thrash, heavier than death metal, it's a genre all its own, strangely beautiful in its psychopathological way, like a Satanic soundtrack. Makes Slayer sound like elevator music.

Code D (For a description of these codes, see "Mailing List Codes" under "Classical Music.")

Owner or Contact Matt Jukins, mpj@kepler.unh.edu

To Subscribe Send a politely worded request to GRIND-Request@unh.edu. To unsubscribe, send a politely worded request to GRIND-Request@unh.edu. Send all articles to GRIND@unh.edu.

Hardcore Punk Music

alt.music.hardcore

One of the very first musical newsgroups, alt.music.hardcore is a great read, but you'll probably want to withhold your contributions until you get a feel for the discussion. The musical menu is first and foremost focused on punk moguls Dead Kennedys, their San Francisco record label Alternative Tentacles, and lead singer Jello Biafra (see also alt.fan.jello.biafra and "Alternative Tentacles Records"). Discussions are impassioned and often profane, and the newbie is flamed alive if he or she dares jump into a discussion without an appreciation for the hardcore scene. While contributors can be pretty brutal at times, they're just writing honestly about music they like: Rancid, Zeni Geva, NoMeansNo— you own all these, right? The punk-vs.-hardcore flamewars only serve to remind subscribers that all other music, well, sucks.

Independent Record Labels

alt.music.independent

Home for devotees of the college-radio scene, this group is a constantly changing source for tour info, release updates, band statuses, and radio programming of independent record-label artists. The roster of bands can differ week by week (Lync, Bikini Kill, Bush, and Rodan featured prominently the last time I checked), but the blood is always fresh in this group. If you like—as I do— the radio stations that play thirty-minute sets of music that your parents always hated, there is no better place on the Net for you than alt.music.independent.

Industrial Music

rec.music.industrial

Whether you're into Skinny Puppy, Pigface, Ministry, Laibach, Neitzer Ebb, LARD, KMFDM, and Front 242, or just want to check out the listings under "Industrial Kink-O-Rama," this is the place for you. Velcome to Schprockets.

Internet Underground Music Archive

http://www.iuma.com/

ftp://ftp.iuma.com

You've read about it in *WIRED* and *Esquire*: The Internet Underground Music Archive (IUMA—pronounced "eye-YOU-ma") is the Net's first and foremost stop for music downloads, info on new bands, GIFs, music and video clips, and a cool new magazine, *Addicted To Noise* (see description in "Calendars and Magazines"). You could easily spend a week at IUMA (see Figure 2.2), checking

Alternative Tentacles Records

A tiny San Francisco record label that has, for fifteen years, promoted truly alternative artists with eye-catching names like Dog-Faced Hermans, Alice Donut, and NoMeansNo, Alternative Tentacles' budding roster varies from jazz to hip-hop to "hardcore" punk. The vision of a hyperactive and dedicated character named Jello Biafra (who led early-80s agitpunk foursome Dead Kennedys), Alternative Tentacles finds the Net one of several effective ways to reach its audience, a combination of punk rockers and DKs fans of all ages.

"We do a huge mail-order business to addresses in midwestern cities," says general manager Greg Werckman, his feet characteristically atop his desk. "I jumped onto the Net a year ago and found that on certain newsgroups, our music was the big topic, with everybody talking about our bands. I decided to start talking back."

From his computer at alt.tent@aol.com, Werckman monitors the alt.punk and alt.music.hardcore newsgroups, reading (and occasionally responding to) listings of info and mis-info that pop up. Although artists on other indie labels such as Amphet-

The internet's first free hi-fi music archive

Figure 2.2 :
The home page for the remarkable
Internet Underground Music
Archive (IUMA), the quintessential
Net musical resource

out bands and downloading audio and graphics files, but with its increased traffic as of late, you may find it best to jump on only occasionally. IUMA updates its files more often than any Website I've found—new listings seem to spring up every week to ten days.

IUMA has begun to receive funding from Warner Brothers, a change that may or may not be a good thing: The best part of the original site was its unapologetic dedication to the underdog artists who took the trouble to submit recordings for public access, and Warner's influence will definitely shift IUMA's balance to feature major artists instead. Such a change is fine if the

amine Reptile and Touch & Go get plenty of interest, Alternative Tentacles is probably the most mentioned label on both those newsgroups, with Biafra the subject of frequent rumor and legend.

"I've read every story about Jello on the Net, and ninety-nine out of a hundred are just speculation," Werckman says. "But I think people realize that just because someone posts something to a newsgroup doesn't make it necessarily true. I respect people all across the world having a chance to write about something they love: Music that's really different."

And AT artists are different: Though you might find LARD or Grotus discussed at rec.music.industrial, Beatnigs or Chill E.B. at alt.rap, or Neurosis at alt.rock–roll.metal, the artists Werckman promotes never sit comfortably under established categories.

"On first-listen or first-see, most of our bands are a little difficult for people to swallow," he admits. "A lot of them have cult followings and people love them or *hate* them. The Internet seems to be a perfect meeting place for everybody to gather and discuss those—um—strong opinions," he grins. "I have nothing against more straight-ahead bands, it's just that Alternative Tentacles has decided to be an outlet for the others."

musical underdogs still have a viable presence; we'll have to see. Regardless, IUMA currently is one of the Net's finest underground musical resources.

IUMA's FTP site offers access to the same information and files as does the website, but no graphics.

As a Net-surfer, you deserve to know how big an audio, video, or graphics file is before you begin downloading it: You may not want to wait as long as it will take. Some WWW browsers indicate the file size (in KB) right next to the icon or file itself; some don't. I think it ought to be a law.

Kosmic Free Music Foundation

http://kosmic.wit.com/~kosmic/

Taking IUMA to task by calling itself the "real" underground music archive, the Kosmic Free Music Foundation maintains a site that features broad access to musical mailing lists, FTP archives, music news (see Figure 2.3), software for playing back audio files, and other utilities. Independently run by a "world-wide group of musicians, artists, programmers, and designers," the KFMF seems interested in challenging IUMA by providing a viable, not-for-profit downloading site for alternative music.

Figure 2.3:
KFMF's Kosmic News logo, found at
http://kosmic.wit.com/~klf/latenews.html.
Click in to the latest in alternative musical headlines.

New Age/Ambient Music

rec.music.newage

"New Age" music used to be synonymous with pianist George Winston and his ilk, but it's come a long way: Artists favored on this stop include performers of "early" music (performed on Baroque period instuments) like Dead Can Dance, commercially successful Enigma, composer Riyuichi Sakamoto, Andreas Vollenweider, Kitaro, and Vangelis. The most talked-about independent labels include Hearts Of Space and Extreme. newage's lengthy discussions range in subject from working definitions of "ambient" to griping about how much "Yanni Sucks." Not too focused yet, but plenty of varied artists and recommendations for interesting music.

New Zealand Pop Bands

KIWIMUSIC

New Zealand is a hotbed of weird and wonderful pop music, including artists like The Chills, The Bats, The Clean, Tall Dwarfs, Peter Jefferies, and Bailter Space, as well as record labels like Flying Nun and Xpressway. This effeciently run mailing list is welcoming and worth checking out.

Owner or Contact Katie Livingston, kiwimusic-request@mit.edu

To Subscribe Send a politely worded request to kiwimusic-request@mit.edu. To unsubscribe, send a politely worded request to kiwimusic-request@mit.edu. Send all articles to KIWIMUSIC@mit.edu.

KIWIMUSIC, *like many mailing lists, refers to itself as a "discussion list." The two terms*—discussion list *and* mailing list—*seem to be interchangeable. Carry on.*

Punk Music

alt.punk

Whereas alt.music.hardcore seems focused on original early-80s punk rock, alt.punk takes the generic term into the present. Punk's not dead, as they say, but has mutated from hardcore roots into broader styles. You'll find info on bands such as New Bomb Turks, Down By Law, GirlsAgainstBoys, and the omnipresent Green Day (who've popularized themselves into the "Rock and Pop" section of this book). There's a directory for subcategories if, for example, you're into straight-edge bands and want a tighter focus to your discussion.

A couple of things I really liked about alt.punk: Occasional discussion topics had multiple posts—like 50 or 60—and I appreciated that the group's moderator let certain threads enjoy the extended spinning they deserve. Also, I drew courage from several book discussions, something most musical newsgroups lack. alt.punk seems dedicated to exploiting young Internet brains, and I appreciate that.

Ska Music

alt.music.ska

The legend behind ska, of course, is that it was replaced by reggae one hot summer when Jamaicans wanted their native music s-l-o-w-e-d down. Discussions at the site verify the music's popularity in both the U.S. and U.K.: Current bands such as Mighty Mighty Bosstones (see listing in "Alternative Music") and Toasters are mentioned alongside such defunct masters as Madness, Specials, and the English Beat. The preponderance of young users makes this newsgroup hospitable and enthusiastic. Oy! Oy! Oy!

Techno Music

alt.music.techno

The techno stop is one of the most focused and most interesting of the music hangouts. It's what a newsgroup should be: Focused enough to define its members yet broad enough in its listings to stay interesting. Plenty of artists' discussion, including FFWD, The KLF, Aphex Twin, and Orbital; lots of access to computer sound files; some equipment for sale or trade; many threads generated about the music itself—what "ambient" is, a good FAQ file, sincere attempts to describe what one hears in techno. Plenty of other newsgroups could benefit from imitating alt.music.techno's example, and although I'm not a huge fan of the genre, I'll be back.

U.K. Independent Record Labels

http://www.crg.cs.nott.ac.uk/~mjr/Music/Alternative/index.html

This site focuses on British techno/rave/dance music, and includes a music 'zine as well as lists of mailing lists that will help you clue in to the scene. The site is small and efficient, and keeps a good U.K. focus: Festivals, readers' polls, and recommended recent releases of a British bent make it an interesting—if esoteric—read, and there are a number of downloadable audio files.

VirtualRadio

http://www.microserve.net/vradio/

I think their name is a little misleading: VirtualRadio (VR, see Figure 2.4) isn't an Internet radio station at all, but rather another database offering audio downloads—whole songs instead of just song samples, some as big as 1-2MB .AU format. (For more information on these formats, see ".AU, .AIFF, .AIFC, .AAAAGH!" in the "Special Collectors' Section.") With artists such as Neurosis, Praxis, and the Chris Cobb Band on their roster, VR culls their sound files from DAT-quality recordings and demonstration tapes. The site experiences occasional bugs (once I got flipped inexplicably into a BBS) but delivers a quality product nonetheless.

As with IUMA, everything on the VirtualRadio site is, if you prefer, accessible via FTP (the URL is listed at their Welcome page).

ALTERNATIVE MUSIC: ARTISTS LISTINGS

Laurie Anderson

alt.fan.laurie.anderson

This inventive vocalist/songstress, who has worked with Peter Gabriel and dozens of other musicians over the years, remains way-wired as ever, releasing brilliant recordings and receiving much adoration on this forum. Her recent tour, the first in several years, re-energized this newsgroup.

Anderson's newsgroup, like all groups related to particular artists, is also called a fan group. There really isn't a difference between the terms, though fan groups seem more like a wired version of old-fashioned fan clubs. Few fan groups are actually set up by the artists themselves; most are just the result of some devotee's hard work.

Figure 2.4:
VirtualRadio's cool logo—not an Internet radio station, but a server where you can download audio files

Bel Canto

BEL-CANTO

A low-volume mailing list of interest to fans of this cerebral Norwegian alternative artist. Former member Geir Jenssen's *Biosphere* project and other members' musical plans take up most of the focused discussion.

Keywords music, Norway, Scandanavia

Owner or Contact Kjetil T. Homme, dewy-fields-request@ifi.uio.no

To Subscribe Send a politely worded request to dewy-fields-request@ifi.uio.no. To unsubscribe, send a politely worded request to dewy-fields-request@ifi.uio.no. Send all articles to dewy-fields@ifi.uio.no.

Jello Biafra

alt.fan.jello.biafra

...as in leader of punk icons Dead Kennedys. Rumors, lies, and actual information about his spoken word tours and his Alternative Tentacles record label. See also alt.music.hardcore and "Alternative Tentacles Records."

Some networks can only access the newsgroup alt.fan.biafra. Try it if you have trouble.

Kate Bush

rec.music.gaffa

I'm not enough of a fan to know where the "gaffa" comes from, but this news-group is dedicated to discussion of siren/singer Kate Bush and similar alternative music. GIFs and films featuring Bush, as well as fans' favorite albums and CDs, cover art, and bootleg recordings feature prominently.

Catherine Wheel

STRANGE-FRUIT

Alternative pop in the Chapterhouse vein, with a mix of young British and American fans; a middle-of-the-road, homogenized grade-A list for Catherine Wheel fans.

Learning to Crawl

There are two ways to browse the Web, and it will help you to be familiar with both: You can do so by using hotlinks (as "A Quick Spin around the Web" showed you in Part One), but you'll often find it easier to simply enter a new URL in order to connect with your chosen destination.

URLs can be tricky to navigate: Start by choosing "New URL" on your browser's menu, and then entering the *entire* URL you're seeking in the space provided. In most cases, just doing that will deliver you—once the browser connects to the appropriate host—to the page you want.

If you receive a message saying your source was "Not Found," however, double-check your typing on the URL. If you've spelled everything correctly, try entering a shorter version of the URL: for example, if you are having trouble with http://www.nando.net/mammoth/chainsaw_kittens.html, just try http://www.nando.net/. Often you can connect to the host with just that information, and can simply add the remaining mammoth/chainsaw_kittens.html once you're at the site.

If you're new to the WWW, you may not realize that particular sites (mammoth's, for example) house many other artists' Web pages. If you don't start at one, try linking to a *Welcome* or *Home page*—the first, most general page on the site, often reached via a link at the bottom of each page. From there, search for broader listings: Bands, record companies, clubs—anything you're looking for that's related to music. If you get lost, your Web browser will always return you to where you started.

Code M, D

Owner or Contact Patty Haley, fruit-request@gdb.org

To Subscribe E-mail fruit-request@gdb.org; in the body of the message, type **SUBSCRIBE STRANGE-FRUIT** followed by your e-mail address. To unsubscribe, send the command **UNSUBSCRIBE STRANGE-FRUIT** in e-mail to · fruit-request@gdb.org. Send all articles to FRUIT@gdb.org.

Chainsaw Kittens

http://www.nando.net/mammoth/chainsaw_kittens.html

With "decadence, charisma, and plenty of good-old-fashioned pop swing," the questionably glam Chainsaw Kittens take to the Net. Snoop around for other artists nearby on the mammoth site.

If you experience repeated problems connecting, try reading "Server Error: <Connection Refused>" in the "Rock and Pop" section of your Pocket Tour.

Danzig

alt.music.danzig

Bad-attitude *rawwwk* fronted by the charismatically Frankensteinian Glen Danzig, popular with the college-radio and alternative crowds.

Dead Can Dance

http://www.nets.com/dcd

I've always liked how Dead Can Dance make use of early musical instruments and sacred vocal style. Once only heard on college radio and in trendy N.Y. lofts, DCD bring their refreshing combination to a new audience on the Net. In addition to earlier recordings (see Figure 2.5), DCD feature their latest release and accompanying film entitled *Toward The Within* at this site. Worth checking out for the sheer beauty of their music.

Aion

1990 - 4AD - CAD 0007 CD

1. The Arrival and the Reunion
2. Saltarello (Instrumental Dance: Anonymous: Italian 14th Century)
3. Mephisto
4. The Song of the Sibyl (Traditional Version: Catalan: 16th Century)
5. Fortune Presents Gifts not According to the Book
6. As the Bell Rings the Maypole Spins
7. The End of Words

Figure 2.5:
The cover of Dead Can Dance's AION CD. The artist brings music performed on early musical instruments to the 20th-century Internet audience.

Devo

alt.fan.devo

Fans of Devo's early 80s spasmo-pop hang out on the Internet, asking the question: *Where are they now?* Leader Mark Mothersbaugh is reportedly writing theme music for children's TV shows and Disney cartoons, but Devo's spud-boy music lives on...on the Internet.

Brian Eno

alt.music.brian-eno

http://www.acns.nwu.edu/eno-1/

The originator of ambience continues to ply interesting material, and here's a great place to stay in touch with it: Eno's newsgroup keeps tabs on the legendary producer/player's every move, whether he's recording for TV ads, appearing on the latest Bryan Ferry or James releases, or lecturing at a nearby university. I'm under the impression that the Website includes a listing of his entire (!) discography, plus biographical and bibliographical sources.

Frente!

http://www.nando.net/mammoth/frente.html

The "antidote to the grunge overload," Frente!'s sparse pop hails from Melbourne, Australia. Another one of the many fine mammoth sites.

PJ Harvey

http://www.louisville.edu/public/jadour01/pjh/

The superb up-and-coming female guitarist and songwriter Polly Jean Harvey, currently supporting her Island release *To Bring You My Love*, (see Figure 2.6) can be found here, along with photos and a biography.

Figure 2.6:
PJ Harvey, guitar in hand, at the Welcome page of her fans' Website

Robyn Hitchcock/Soft Boys

FEGMANIAX

Robyn Hitchcock began as one of the punk Soft Boys and soon embarked on a successful solo career constructed of clever pop musings. Less prolific than he once was—with over a dozen releases to his name—he still provides plenty of fodder for his Internet FEGMANIAX.

Code D

Owner or Contact Woj, woj@remsu.rutgers.edu

To Subscribe Send a politely worded request to fegmaniax-request@gnu.ai.mit.edu. To unsubscribe, send a politely worded request to fegmaniax-request@gnu.ai.mit.edu. Send all articles to FEGMANIAX@gnu.ai.mit.edu.

King Crimson/Robert Fripp

http://www.cs.man.ac.uk/aig/staff/toby/discipline.html

Formerly called "Discipline," the "Elephant Talk" newsletter is archived here for fans of the experimental guitarist Fripp and his timeless King Crimson combo.

Level 42

LEVEL42

There isn't much dance music to choose from in the mailing lists section, but the exception is Level 42, a long-time survivor of the industrial genre. This list is popular with both European and American subscribers.

Code D

Owner or Contact Eric J. Hansen, eric@enterprise.bih.harvard.edu

To Subscribe E-mail level42-request@enterprise.bih.harvard.edu; in the body of the message, type **SUBSCRIBE**. To unsubscribe, send the command **UNSUB-SCRIBE** to level42-request@enterprise.bih.harvard.edu. Send all articles to LEVEL42@enterprise.bih.harvard.edu.

Mighty Mighty Bosstones

http://crow.acns.nwu.edu:8080/bosstones

A site for one of the most popular bands in the skanking business right now, this page for Boston's Mighty Mighty Bosstones includes a discography, tour info, and lyrics to a few songs (see alt.music.ska earlier in this section for more ska bands).

Misfits

http://watt.seas.virginia.edu/~msk4m/

Unlike "generation X," this isn't a lifestyle choice: Rather, a funny, lo-fi Web page for the original punk-ghoul band The Misfits. Includes lyrics, discography, and guitar chord listings for their songs.

Nine Inch Nails

alt.music.nin

One of the hottest and fastest-growing fan groups, the Nine Inch Nails' site includes every frightening, fascinating, and grisly detail that NIN fans care to share about the band, including interpretations for their own sticky dreams about lead singer Trent Reznor. You'll also find news about NIN's relations with super-industrial group Ministry, their Halo record label, or the promised "true meaning" of the band's name. This band is so big I had to include them in the "Rock and Pop" section, too.

If you're so inclined (and your system administrator lets you access it), check out alt.sex.fetish.trent.reznor. *Maybe this Tip should be a Warning instead....*

Pop Will Eat Itself

alt.music.pop.will.eat.itself

http://kzsu.stanford.edu/uwi/pwei/pwei.html

Political, beat-heavy British dance music, PWEI—yes, it's a band—has a small but devoted following. Mailing lists, tour info, and discussions of other bands PWEI fans might like (Wonder Stuff, for example) fill in the newsgroup's listings; the Website offers an even more complete listing, with graphics.

They Might Be Giants

alt.music.tmbg

Once upon a time, two guys named John made songs using only a drum machine, an electric guitar, and a whiny accordion. Everyone thought They Might Be Giants were weird—and they still are, they're just huge now. The best FAQ file I've seen, information on their legendary dial-a-song, and numerous anagrams—some crude, some cryptic, some intriguing—for their name. Not deep, but fun.

Frank Zappa

alt.fan.frank-zappa

http://www.fwi.uva/nl/~heederik/zappa/

The remarkably prolific presidential candidate and gonzo songwriter probably lived to see the creation of his fan group, whose members are clever and pleasantly demented. The Website, based in Amsterdam, houses "St. Alphonso's Pancake Homepage" (see Figure 2.7).

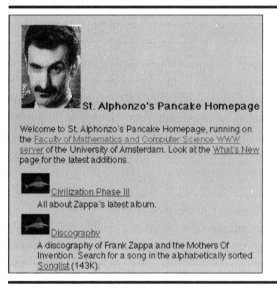

Figure 2.7:
St. Alphonso's Pancake Homepage, one of several sources for information on music of the late, great Frank Zappa

ALTERNATIVE MUSIC: RECORD COMPANIES

American Recordings

http://american.recordings.com

Among the best sources for Internet music, Rick Rubin's record company (see Figure 2.8) maintains a stunningly complete and frequently updated Website, one of the most interesting I've found. Whether you're seeking a huge listing

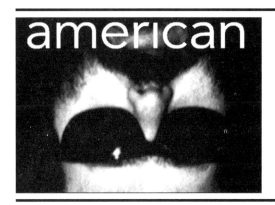

Figure 2.8:
The inverted founder of
American Recordings, Rick Rubin

of bands, record labels (see "Record Label Listings"), lists of music-related mailing lists, or radio stations that maintain Websites, American's "World Wide Web of Music" and "Major Music Links" (see Figure 2.9) are central switching-yards for much of the rest of the musical Internet.

Check out info for Lollapalooza '95; download from hundreds of graphics and audio files; search for your favorite artist, classified by genre and alphabetized (see Figure 2.10). Definitely worth your while; nice to see an industry site that does so much. American's site is the four-star winner for the Alternative Music section.

Figure 2.9:
American's WWW of Music, a remarkably complete Internet music source

Figure 2.10:
Search for your favorite artist alphabetically on
American's "Ultimate Band List Searcher."

Mammoth Records

http:www.nando.net/mammoth

With a roster of artists including Charlie Hunter Trio, Blake Babies, Alphabet Soup, Victoria Williams, and Eskimo, Mammoth houses a broad variety of underexposed genres, from jazz to punk to other alternatives, all up-'n'-coming acts you're sure to hear about soon. Check out the link to Prawn Song, Primus bassist Les Claypool's own label. Only one thing: Occasionally, this site can be difficult to access.

Seventh Heaven Records

http://www.pacificrim.net:80/~7heaven/

This tiny label hailing from rural Bellingham, WA strives to promote Pacific Northwest bands. A typical example of a good homegrown Web page, the site contains simple graphics and eye-catching, easily manipulated interfaces—and was accessible every time I tried. Currently hyping a band called Black.

Sub Pop Records

http://www.subpop.com/

A recent addition to the Web, the Sub Pop stop is home to many, many great new acts, including Combustible Edison, Red Red Meat, Pond, the Reverend Horton Heat, and others. Oh, yeah: Sub Pop also released the first records by a then-unknown band called "Nirvana," who went on to become pretty famous.

Windham Hill Records

http://www.windham.com

True, you'll find standby artists such as Michael Hedges, Modern Mandolin Quartet, and George Winston (whose best-selling recordings put this Northern California record label on the map nearly twenty years ago), but check out Windham Hill's more recent additions at a friendly and easy-to-navigate home page (see Figure 2.11). Their High Street sub-label link features lesser-known artists such as Jazz Passengers, subdudes, and Tuck & Patti; also track down their sheet music, songbooks, extremely cool by-state radio station guide, and chat line. Very up on the times, the Windham Hill site is an excellent stop.

Figure 2.11:
Windham Hill's home page, simple and easy to navigate. You'll be glad you have a color monitor.

ALTERNATIVE MUSIC: DANCE LISTINGS

Northeast Raves

NERaves

For northeastern North America (from Chicago east, DC north, and eastern Canadian provinces), NERaves is the source for the blissed-out marathon music/club/dance scene, primarily as a billboard for upcoming events.

Code U

Contact ne-raves-request@silver.lcs.mit.edu (John Adams)

Southeast US Raves

SERAVES

Dedicated to techno music and the rave scene, particularly in the Southeastern U.S., SERAVES differs from NERaves in that it promotes itself as a chatty, free-form list, encouraging reviews of music, raves, DJs, and clubs, as well as announcements of upcoming events.

Keywords Rave, Southeast, techno, music, reviews, clubs, announcements

Owner or Contact John Humphrey, jrhumphr@eos.ncsu.edu; Derek Tiffany, tiffanyde@urvax.urich.edu; Doug Zimmerman, DZ5401a@american.edu

To Subscribe E-mail LISTSERV@AMERICAN.EDU; in the body of the message type **SUBSCRIBE SERAVES** followed by your full name. To unsubscribe, send the command **UNSUB SERAVES** in e-mail to LISTSERV@AMERICAN.EDU. Send all other list-related commands to LISTSERV@AMERICAN.EDU. Send **HELP** for a list of available commands. Send articles to SERAVES@AMERICAN.EDU.

Record Label Listings

Here's a complete list of the record labels currently accessible through http://american.recordings.com:

American Recordings

Bad Taste Ltd

Bedazzled Records

Beyond Records

Black Boot Records

Black Rock Coalition

Breakfast Records

C/Z Records

Catasonic

Charnel Music

Discography of 4AD, by group

East Side Digital Music

Eat Me Recordings

Editions de la Rue Margo (Paris)

Enemy Records

Etiquette Records

Flat Field Records

Geffen/DGC Records

go kart Records

Grand Royal

Heyday Records

IWanna Records

Kaleidospace Music Kiosk

Landphil Records

Mammoth Records

Metropolis Records

Motown

N-Fusion Records

Nettwerk

PrettyBoy Records

Quagmire

Rage Records

Revelation Records

Rhino Records

Silent Records America

Sony Music

SubPop

TeenBeat

Triloka Records/Worldly Music

Warner Brothers

Windham Hill

World Domination

ZoeMagik Records

...pretty impressive, and sure to be adding more soon.

Classical Music

The Internet is making great progress as a tool for the online classical music enthusiast—the record collector, the symphonic musician, the researcher—with readily available archives for libraries, discographies, music, and organizational services.

The Internet isn't like an apartment building where you have to deal with your noisy neighbors. It can, perhaps to the preference of most classical music fans, be a delightfully silent place, an intimate setting for concentrated research and quiet discovery. In comparison to the Alternative Music surfer, you may prefer to travel online in utter soundlessness, winding down glimmering cyberavenues of digital beauty, unencumbered by soundbytes of Smashing Pumpkins or Nine Inch Nails.

Classical music is one of the fastest-growing music genres on the Net: If you're one of its aficionados, why not consider starting your own mailing list, newsgroup, or Web page, for the collective benefit of colleagues who, like you, surf the Net in black tie and tails?

CLASSICAL MUSIC: GENERAL LISTINGS

American String Teachers Association

ASTA-L

Aimed at subscribers from grade school music teachers to symphony musicians, the ASTA-L list includes detailed discussions on string pedagogy, students' repertoire and performance, and pertinent announcements from members of American String Teachers Association, the newsgroup's founding organization.

Code U (For a description of these codes, see "Mailing List Codes" later in this section.)

Owner or Contact Michael Bersin, mb0458@cmsuvmb.cmsu.edu

To Subscribe E-mail LISTSERV@cmsuvmb.cmsu.edu; in the body of the message, type **SUBSCRIBE ASTA-L** followed by your real name. To unsubscribe, send the command **UNSUBSCRIBE ASTA-L** in e-mail to LISTSERV@cmsuvmb.cmsu.edu. Send all other list-related commands to LISTSERV@cmsuvmb.cmsu.edu. For assistance, send the command **HELP**. Send all articles containing more than 200 lines to the list owner; all others to ASTA-L@cmsuvmb.cmsu.edu.

Classical Guitar Fans and Players

rec.music.classical.guitar

Fluent in Flamenco? Mason Williams? Villa-Lobos? This group's discussion is diverse: Warm-up exercises, favorite pieces to play, and finger-picking tips address technique; other topics include female guitarists, publications of interest, teaching assistantships, for-sales, and recommended schools for the young player. The discussion comparing the benefits of gut and nylon strings could also occur in a **sports.tennis** newsgroup, I suppose, but I'll bet **rec.music.classical. guitar** is the only musical forum with listings on fingernail condition.

Your best starting place in the "Classical Music" section is the following newsgroup. Have fun!

Classical Music

rec.music.classical

As you'd expect, **rec.music.classical** is a huge newsgroup, where you can find nearly any musical information you need—as long as it has to do with classical music. Strictly speaking, it's devoted primarily to recordings: Sales, re-releases, rarities, movie soundtracks, and discographies, all classical in focus. But you'll also find plenty of info about conducting workshops, classical melody studies, and festivals in the spaces between recording discussions.

rec.music.classical's most popular threads include Beethoven piano sonatas, the opera *Carmina Burana*, last year's *Three Tenors* release (featuring Carreras, Domingo, and Pavarotti in a recording not highly favored by this forum), endless threads concerning classical pieces that make you cry with joy or sorrow, and suggested honeymoon CDs. I read posts between a 15-year-old novice violinist and a symphony conductor, both of whom seemed entirely comfortable here.

If you're unfamiliar with terms like thread *and* post, *check the "Newsgroup Glossary" in the "Alternative Music" section.*

Classical Music Reviews

http://www.ncsa.uiuc.edu/SDG/People/marca/music-reviews.html

Sounds like a man with lots of time on his hands: Proprietor Dave Lampson's reviews and recommendations of his favorite Baroque, Classical, Romantic, and Modern recordings.

Current Opera

http://www.webcom.com:80/~redwards/welcome.html

Proprietor Richard Edwards has a clearly-stated purpose for maintaining this Website, as he tells you himself: To get you to go to the opera. Edwards' love for the libretta began as the OPERA-L mailing list, archived at http://web.metronet/elektra/operal.html and easily reached via this site (see Figure 2.12). OPERA-L became the *Current Opera Digest*, which in turn hatched the "What is Current Opera?" Website. For the opera fan or the uninitiated, this site is a must-stop, with reviews and previews of famous performances, a calendar of events for the Portland/Seattle opera community, and megabytes of information on the life of Giovanni Bottesini, Edwards' hero. You can also link to several other opera-based Websites from here. Lots of work put in by a true enthusiast.

Opera-L Pictures, Biographies, & More	Figure 2.12: Art from Opera-L Pictures, archived at http://web.metronet/elektra/operal.html, and easily reached through Richard Edwards' Current Opera Web page

KDFC Classical Radio

http://www.tbo.com/kdfc/index.html

At the Website for one of the few online classical radio stations, you can learn about San Francisco-based KDFC itself, sign up for a copy of the station's *Classic Notes* newsletter, and check out its hotlinks to other classically-related artists, newsgroups, and archive sites, including the San Jose Symphony Orchestra (which also appears in this section).

Having trouble manipulating URLs? You can get help by reading "Learning to Crawl" in the "Alternative Music" section.

Lesbian and Gay Chorus

CHORUS

Besides focusing on gay and lesbian choral groups and their music and repertoire, CHORUS also contains discussions about related matters, including administration, concert production, staging, and fundraising. Self-described as having a "friendly and social atmosphere," CHORUS appears to attract members who are hospitable and hard-working.

Owner or Contact Brian A. Jarvis, jarvis@psych.toronto.edu, John Schrag, jschrag@alias.com

To Subscribe Send a politely worded request to CHORUS-Request@psych.toronto.edu. To unsubscribe, send a politely worded request to CHORUS-Request@psych.toronto.edu. Send all articles to CHORUS@psych.toronto.edu.

Music Library Distribution

IAML-L

See description in "Musicians' Resources."

San Jose Symphony Orchestra

http://webcom.com/~sjsympho/

With its audience based in the heart of Silicon Valley, the San Jose Symphony Orchestra, if any, should have an online presence. The SJSO's is excellent: Upcoming concerts   (including their popular Signature Series), profiles,

Mailing List Codes

M usical mailing lists vary from once-a-month publications to up-to-the-minute, hundred-post accounts of tours in progress. The codes (D, M, U) that follow the list descriptions correspond to universal variations, not just those in this book.

Code D: Many lists send out a compilation of several days' or weeks' articles in
Digest option digest form. Because you receive several pieces in one mailing, this option is valuable if you have to pay for e-mail by the piece. Also, packing a newsletter up into a collection of articles allows for fewer electronic mis-deliveries; it's like shipping a crate of cantaloupes instead of two dozen single ones.

Most lists are receivable as a digest. Double-check your subscription confirmation (the first mailing you receive after a subscription request) or send a request to the list manager. Especially with larger lists, taking this simple step makes your life a lot easier.

biographies, and pictures of their musicians, and an in-depth section featuring music director and conductor Leonid Grin fill out the site nicely. You can even download music samples, from Schubert to Tchaikovsky to Billy Strayhorn's "Take the A Train." Classy and classical.

Symphonic Musicians

rec.music.classical.performing

Fortified with an occasional debate between conductors, performers, and composers, this newsgroup is a comprehensive one for symphony musicians. You'll find discussions about every conceivable instrument in the orchestra—including car horns—as well as recommendations for playing techniques and instrument repair, cleaning, and upkeep. Every line of work should have access to this kind of support.

Code M: **A** moderated list employs an editor who makes content decisions to
Moderated ensure that the forum stays focused and concise. Huge, ungainly fan mail-
list ing lists are often moderated, and that's probably good for keeping the gibberish down. But the Net doesn't like denial of access to information, and moderated lists occasionally smack of censorship.

When you decide to post something to a list, be sure to send it to the *articles* address, not the subscriptions address. If the list is moderated, and you think you're getting crowded out or censored, think about starting your own.

Code U: Moderated lists run everything that's sent them, and seem more frequently
Unmoderated used with esoteric subjects. Sometimes, in the face of trouble, an unmod-
list erated list will convert to a moderated one; as Net traffic increases exponentially, that may happen more often.

CLASSICAL MUSIC: COMPOSERS AND PERFORMERS LISTINGS

Gustav Mahler Symphonies

http://www.ncsa.uiuc.edu/SDG/People/marca/barker-mahler.html

This Web page features a lengthy, text-based discussion on the subject by Deryk Barker, with a remarkable accompanying discography.

I've had a hard time locating many classical audio files online, which is no surprise: It's much easier to load a three-minute Green Day soundbyte than a Copeland symphony. Nonetheless, if you snoop around http://www.vng.unit. no:80/songs/bach.html, *you might—that's* might—*find a snippet of Bach: When I last checked, this site was still under construction, with no files yet available, but since our medium is the Internet, things could well have changed.*

Vangelis

DIRECT

http://bau2.uibk.ac.at/perki/Vangelis.html

Devoted to the compositions of pianist and composer Evangelos O. Papathanassiou—no wonder he chose "Vangelis"—this fan list discusses both his work as a composer and his life, his old and new recordings, and includes tangential topics such as synthesizer techniques and technologies as they relate to his music.

Code D

Owner or Contact Keith Gregoire, keith@celtech.com

To Subscribe Send a politely worded request to direct-request@celtech.com. To unsubscribe, send a politely worded request to direct-request@celtech.com. Send all articles to DIRECT@celtech.com.

CLASSICAL MUSIC: DANCE LISTINGS

Ballroom and Swing Dancing

BALLROOM

The ballroom list offers information on clubs and other places to dance, dancing types, steps, technique, and etiquette, as well as providing sources for ballroom dance music. Brush up before that wedding....

Owner or Contact Shahrukh Merchant, BALLROOM-Request@mitvma.mit.edu

To Subscribe E-mail LISTSERV@mitvma.mit.edu; in the body of the message, type **SUBSCRIBE BALLROOM** followed by your real name. To unsubscribe, send the command **UNSUBSCRIBE BALLROOM** in e-mail to LISTSERV@mitvma. mit.edu. Send all other list-related commands to LISTSERV@mitvma.mit.edu. For assistance, send the command **HELP**. Send all articles to BALLROOM@mitvma.mit.edu.

Folk and Country Music

The Internet seems, at first glance, to be a medium that would attract computer musicians wielding electronic keyboards and digital samplers, one with no room for the country folks with their acoustic instruments and simpler preferences. But don't forget, the Internet is a community where everyone has an equal voice: For that reason, you may find that rolling along the Net's dusty backroads—that parallel the superhighway where everyone with California plates is doing 85 MPH—in search of country and folk music might be much more your speed.

Like classical music, folk and country are two genres that have just begun to boom on the Net: Whether you're looking for your favorite artist's fan club or fiddle strings, you'll have better and better luck finding it online. If you're a musician, don't forget to check the "Musicians' Resources" section for information on festivals, techniques, and hard-to-find parts for your particular instrument.

FOLK AND COUNTRY: GENERAL LISTINGS

Country Western Music

rec.music.country.western

Ever notice how country-western stars are instantly recognizable by just their first names? You can find the fans of Garth, Tami, Wynonna, Billy Ray, Lyle, Merle, Dolly, and Hank hanging out here, trading line-dancing techniques and bits of trivia. Plenty of equipment for sale, as well as hundreds of concert dates listed. Newer country acts such as kd lang and Jimmie Dale Gilmore get less attention than the big stars, but given the crossover of a major country artist such as Johnny Cash into college radio these days, I'd bet their time will come.

Folk/Bluegrass/Celtic DJs

FOLKDJ-L

I can't differentiate between Flatt-and-Scruggs' style and melodic bluegrass, but subscribers to this list probably can. Overlapping topics include folk, bluegrass, and Celtic music, plus ideas on fundraising, record company relations, and community outreach. "Not limited to DJs," they say; open to anyone at the hoe-down.

Keywords music, folk, bluegrass, Celtic, radio

Owner or Contact Tina Hay, tmh1@psuvm.psu.edu

To Subscribe E-mail LISTSERV@psuvm.psu.edu; in the body of the message, type **SUBSCRIBE FOLKDJ-L** followed by your real name. To unsubscribe, send the command **UNSUB FOLKDJ-L** in e-mail to LISTSERV@psuvm.psu.edu. Send all other list-related commands to LISTSERV@psuvm.psu.edu. Send all articles to FOLKDJ-L@psuvm.psu.edu.

Folk Music

rec.music.folk

Leonard Cohen, John Prine, and Pete Seeger match up with Mary Chapin Carpenter, Nanci Griffith, and Maria Muldaur. The sexes are in balance elsewhere on rec.music.folk as well: Multiple listings for the Indigo Girls and Iris Dement fan clubs balance a large listing for "Best Gordon Lightfoot Song."

For folkies, either the rec.music.folk *newsgroup or* FOLKTALK *list are good starting places; for the country fan, try the* rec.music.country.western *newsgroup.*

FOLKTALK

FOLKTALK defines its genre as "purebred American mongrel music," sneaking it from the backwoods of folk a little closer to rock-and-roll. Discussion topics range from Bela Fleck to De Dannan, from New Age to "almost jazz."

Code U (For a description of these codes, see "Mailing List Codes" in "Classical Music.")

Owner or Contact Scott "Aging Folkie" Hammer, scoth@wmvm1.cc.wm.edu

To Subscribe E-mail LISTSERV@wmvm1.cc.wm.edu; in the body of the message, type **SUBSCRIBE FOLKTALK** followed by your real name. To unsubscribe, send the command **UNSUBSCRIBE FOLKTALK** in e-mail to LISTSERV@wmvm1.cc.wm.edu. Send all other list-related commands to LISTSERV@wmvm1.cc.wm.edu. For assistance, send the command **HELP**. Send all articles to FOLKTALK@wmvm1.cc.wm.edu.

Nashville Net

http://www.nashville.net/

One of the recommended stops from Curb Records, this site gives the visitor plenty of history and recommended sights and sounds around Nashville.

FOLK AND COUNTRY: ARTISTS LISTINGS

Suzy Bogguss

http://www.dur.ac.uk/~d3g6cj/suzy.html

With eight LPs to her name, this deserving star has a Web page filled with fan club info, lyrics, and loads of pictures, facts, and trivia.

Garth Brooks

http://www.tecc.co.uk/mparkes/docs/garthpic.html

As of this writing, the country mega-star's Web page includes only photos (see Figure 2.13) and some guitar tabulature for a few songs.

Mary Chapin Carpenter

http://www.cis.ohio-state.edu/~juliano/robpage/mcc.music.html

This Website houses her complete discography with plans for fanclub information, photos, and more.

Figure 2.13:
Unexpected guest: Garth Brooks on the Internet,
downloaded from his Web page

Johnny Cash

http://american.recordings.com/cgi-bin/ubl?card+2369

Wish I could say that Cash's Website is fantastic, but I had repeated trouble accessing it. I hope that changes, because The Man in Black is an American legend who deserves the kind of exposure the Internet provides.

Bob Dylan

rec.music.dylan

I find it wonderful that fans of Bob Dylan—probably some of the last people you'd expect to be wired—keep a fan group for him on the Internet.

Eagles

http://www.coc.powell-river.bc.ca/eagles/eagles.html

The dinosaurs of country-rock (they began in 1971), the Eagles are big on the Web, too, with a hugely graphic Website featuring dozens of photos, lyrics, history, concert reviews, and biographies of Glenn Frey, Don Henley, Joe Walsh, and other past Eaglets. Their recent tour, the first in years, re-energized interest on the site.

Bela Fleck and the Flecktones

alt.music.bela-fleck

With influences of both bluegrass and country, banjo-playin' Bela is popular with a broad cross-section of fans.

Dan Fogelberg

FOGELBERG

Singer-songwriter Fogelberg is still a favorite among many folk music fans; his list is a medium-sized stop.

Owner or Contact Beverly Woolf, bwoolf@pro-woolf.clark.net

To Subscribe E-mail bwoolf@pro-woolf.clark.net; in the body of the message, type **SUBSCRIBE FOGELBERG** followed by your real name. To unsubscribe, send the command **UNSUBSCRIBE FOGELBERG** in e-mail to bwoolf@pro-woolf.clark.net. Send all articles to FOGELBERG@pro-woolf.clark.net.

news.announce.newgroups

If you're a folkie (or a fan of any kind of music) who wants your finger on the pulse of the newest news, the grooviest groups, and the freshest forums, click into news.announce.newgroups: In this group you'll find *RFD*s—Requests For Discussion, *CFV*s—Calls For Vote, voting results, new mailing lists, and other announcements affecting the mushrooming newsgroup field.

One of this forum's most-read listings is the "Guidelines For Usenet Group Creation," a schematic for creating a newsgroup. This procedure starts with a posted "Request For Discussion" in news.announce.newgroups and any other groups or mailing lists related to the proposed topic, and follows a specific process to predetermine its chances for success.

A typical sampling of the music-related items on news.announce.newgroups:

- An RFD for the creation of three new newsgroups aimed at members of high school and collegiate marching bands, their faculty, and supporters. The charter proposes listings for upcoming competitions, events, and information about equipment.

- An RFD for rec.music.funky.rap, an unmoderated newsgroup for "the discus-

Nanci Griffith

http://www.nvg.unit.no/~paul/nanci/nanci1.html

This singer-songwriter grows ever-more popular with every release, and her Website is filled with all the facts, photos, and song lyrics her fans want.

Roy Harper

stormcock

stormcock is actually the site for folk-rock musician Harper, whose politically-conscious music finds a small and loyal following on the Internet. Some users may have to route mail through the U.K. Internet gateway nsfnet-relay.ac.uk.

Contact stormcock-request@dcs.qmw.ac.uk (Paul Davison)

---

sion and dissemination of information specifically relating to hip-hop music and culture." rec.music.funky forum members interested in rap music evidently feel the genre generates enough traffic in its discussion to justify its own newsgroup. Vote is upcoming.

- An announcement for ORCHESTRALIST, a mailing list for orchestral conductors and those in the orchestra business.

- A last call for votes on unmoderated rec.music.makers.bands, a newsgroup "open to discussion on all topics of interest to a musician who plays in a band." Passage requires 2/3 vote by interested parties. (The vote later passes by 205 to 30.)

- An announcement of the creation of a Bon Jovi mailing list.

- An announcement of rec.music.classical.recordings, a new newsgroup.

- An RFD for rec.music.country.old-time, music from the "southern Appalachian region of Virginia, North Carolina, West Virginia, Kentucky, and Tennessee.... Topics of discussion may include fiddle tunes, banjo tunes, instruments and instrument techniques...."

Sophie Hawkins

alt.music.sophie-hawkins

The self-described "omni-sexual" poetic singer is often familiar to fans of other female songwriters Tori Amos, Kate Bush, and Sara McLachlan—all of whose names come up in the posts—and her newsgroup is intimate and friendly.

Indigo Girls

INDIGO-GIRLS

Indigo Girls' refreshing folk attracts a predominantly female audience, and their Net mailing list is small and intimate. Lots of intelligent discussion centered on their music, but reaching in many directions.

Code D

Owner or Contact Alan Dorn Hetzel, dorn@indigo.mese.com

To Subscribe E-mail indigo-girls-request@indigo.mese.com; in the body of the message, type **SUBSCRIBE INDIGO-GIRLS** followed by your real name. To unsubscribe, send the command **UNSUBSCRIBE INDIGO-GIRLS** in e-mail to indigo-girls-request@indigo.mese.com. Send all other list-related commands to indigo-girls-request@indigo.mese.com. Send all articles to INDIGO-GIRLS@indigo.mese.com.

Kimberly M'Carver

http://www.phoenix.net/~nishimi/mcarver.html

With two releases on Rounder Records (see Figure 2.14), this folk singer appeared recently at Austin, Texas' South-By-Southwest Music Conference (see "Calendar and Magazines"), a meeting of the brightest new stars in the music scene—country, folk, or otherwise.

Reba McEntire

http://ruby.ph.utexas.edu/RebaWWW/Reba.html

Find out all about Reba's diet, Grammy nominations, and appearances in upcoming TV mini-series, as well as lyrics and reviews from her many records.

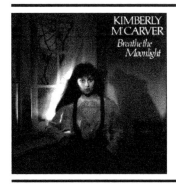
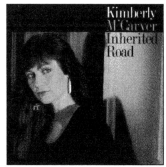

Figure 2.14:
Kimberly M'Carver's
site features images of
both her Rounder
Records releases.

John Mellencamp

http://www.cs.cmu.edu:8001/afs/andrew/usr/da2x/mosaic/mellencamp.html

John Cougar? John Mellencamp? John Cougar Mellencamp? All one and the
same, all found here.

Poi Dog Pondering

POI-POUNDERS

Once the darlings of the collegiate radio set, this odd folk/rock collision hasn't
released records for a while, but their Net address is humming. Happy music,
happy listings.

Code D

Owner or Contact John Relph, poi-pounders-request@presto.ig.com

To Subscribe E-mail poi-pounders-request@presto.ig.com; in the body of the
message, type **SUBSCRIBE POI-POUNDERS** followed by your e-mail address
and real name. To unsubscribe, send the command **UNSUBSCRIBE POI-
POUNDERS** in e-mail to poi-pounders-request@presto.ig.com. Send all other list-
related commands to poi-pounders-request@presto.ig.com. Information on where
to send articles will be sent upon subscribing.

*The POI-POUNDERS list is one of the first I ever found on the Internet; it
seems to be destined to last longer than the band itself.*

Uncle Tupelo

http://www2.ncsu.edu/eos/users/s/sdhouse/Mosaic/uncle-tupelo.html

With lyrics, guitar tabulature, and a few pictures, this Web page is devoted to the remarkable country/college rockers Uncle Tupelo, who split up last year after four successful releases. It's a lo-fi site, friendly and simple. Look for former UT members in another group, Wilco, also discussed at this site.

Jerry Jeff Walker

http://c4sys.hqpacaf.af.mil/hood/music/Jerry.Jeff

I had some initial trouble accessing this site, but eventually it unfolded into a good source for biography, discography, and a few pieces of artwork.

Wild Colonials

http://www.nando.net/music/gm/WildColonials/

A funny, friendly, personal page from this country outfit.

FOLK AND COUNTRY: RECORD COMPANIES

Curb Records

http://www.curb.com/

"At the Curb of the information superhighway," claims the initial text, lies an excellent source for fans of Lyle Lovett, Merle Haggard, Sawyer Brown, Wynnona Judd, Delbert McClinton, and many other stars. This record company's home page features an online catalogue, tour itineraries, and many other links to favorite country Internet resources. Despite being occasionally difficult to tap into, Curb is well worth the time spent getting there. Check out their "Step Off the Curb" link to other musical stops.

Jazz, R & B, and Rap Music

Definitely a scene to watch, the Internet's groove section is slowly expanding to match the exponential growth of online resources. It frustrates me to combine such divergent types of music under one heading, but traveling the Internet, I've found that jazz, rap, and rhythm-and-blues listings tend to overlap. A perfect example is longtime funk king George Clinton, whose recent forays into rap prove the capabilities of established music genres to jump to new mediums; Clinton is the subject of several entries in this section.

Of the three genres, jazz seems to be the fastest-growing, with Blue Note, acid, and hip-hop-jazz listings leading the pack; but rap and hip-hop are booming as well, and while old-school acts like Run-DMC and commercial successes like the Beastie Boys seem the most likely to pop up, keep your eyes peeled for many, many more. Fueled by renewed interest in vintage funk (thanks to Dr. Funkenstein), R & B shows slow, steady growth. Whether you're a rhythm-and-blues fan or a straight-no-chaser jazzbeau, you might experience some frustration tracking down that rare vinyl through Websites or artists' fan groups: Why not consider starting one of your own?

JAZZ, R & B, AND RAP: GENERAL LISTINGS

Acid Jazz and Related Music

ACID-JAZZ

A blend of hip-hop, be-bop, and funk, acid is the fastest-growing jazz genre in the world and on the Net, and includes artists such as Groove Collective, MC Solaar, United Future Organization, and Brand New Heavies. Its list provides a critical source of information on releases and concerts, record labels such as

Ubiquity, Luv 'N' Haight, and Talkin' Loud, acid-jazzy magazines and interviews, and lots of discussion about the San Francisco scene.

Code M (For a description of these codes, see "Mailing List Codes" under "Classical Music.")

Owner or Contact Greg B. Beuthin, gregbb@uhunix.uhcc.hawaii.edu

To Subscribe E-mail LISTSERV@ucsd.edu; in the body of the message, type **ADD** followed by your e-mail address and **ACID-JAZZ**. To unsubscribe, send the command **UNSUBSCRIBE ACID-JAZZ** in e-mail to LISTSERV@ucsd.edu. Send all other list-related commands to LISTSERV@ucsd.edu. For assistance, send the command **HELP**. Send all articles to ACID-JAZZ@ucsd.edu.

This section offers several excellent starting places: If you're interested in acid jazz, either the ACID-JAZZ *list or acid jazz Website (the next entry) will send you in the right direction; for straight jazz, try the* rec.music.bluenote *newsgroup; for blues, I would suggest the* BLUES-L *list; if you're into hip-hop, either the* funky *list or newsgroup will help. Of all the* Pocket Tour *sections, "Jazz, R & B, Rap" is the best for newbies.*

Acid Jazz Server

http://www.cmd.uu.se/AcidJazz/

With acid jazz all the rage these days, it's rewarding to find a simple and tidy site that explains the phenomenon to the uninitiated: Starting with sections titled "What is Acid Jazz?" and "Where did it come from?", followed by a remarkable number of examples, magazines, clubs, and originators of the genre, you'll leave the site with a much clearer definition—and a definite appetite—for this groove. See you at the Elbo Room.

BlueNote Jazz

rec.music.bluenote

The jazz-and-blues Net source, rec.music.bluenote takes on all discussion of the ever-changing American genre. From Grover Washington Jr. and Art Tatum, Chick Corea to Marsalis brothers Wynton and Branford, from Ornette Coleman to Steely Dan, there's something here for everyone. Great jazz quotes and trivia, and discussions ranging from hard bop definitions to chord-scale relation-ships. It wouldn't surprise me, with the renewed interest in jazz as well as the huge traffic of rap and hip-hop listings, if this group splintered some day into several, but for the time being, it's excellent. Somehow, I can't imagine rec.music.bluenote users surfing the Net at night—not until smoky clubs offer a dollar-per-hour public Internet link.

Blues Music

BLUES-L

A list for the discussion of an original American musical form, Blues-L focuses on blues music and its performers, from Blind Blake and Charley Patton to Robert Cray and Stevie Ray Vaughan, as well as any related topics. From back-woods Delta to backstreets Chicago, this list is deep, deep blue.

Code U

Owner or Contact David Pimmel, pimmel@cs.wisc.edu, William Williams, William_Williams.lotus@crd.lotus.com.

To Subscribe E-mail LISTSERV@brownvm.brown.edu; in the body of the message, type **SUBSCRIBE BLUES-L** followed by your real name. To unsubscribe, send the command **UNSUBSCRIBE BLUES-L** to LISTSERV@brownvm.brown.edu. Send all other commands to LISTSERV@brownvm.brown.edu. Send all articles to BLUES-L@brownvm.brown.edu.

BluesNet

http://dragon.acadiau.ca/~rob/blues/

This under-construction site is broken into several sections: "Artist Summaries," "Picture Archives," and "Mentors," with introduction screens to guide you. I liked the "Delta Snake Blues News" link (if not just for the name alone) and the link to "Center for the Study of Southern Culture"—as impor-tant a subject to blues as the music itself.

Funky Music

rec.music.funky

This fast-growing newsgroup trying to encompass "funk, rap, hip-hop, house, soul, and r&b" could well split into several, all of which would boast massive popularity. US3, Spearhead, Bernie Worrell, Groove Collective, and the Meters get their share of discussion, yet the biggest draws are still the P-Funk discography and endless posts about George Clinton and Bootsy Collins. Acid jazz isn't specifically covered under the umbrella of suggested genres, but gets plenty of attention here as well.

FUNKY-MUSIC

Based on the rhythmic innovations pioneered by James Brown, the mix is broad on FUNKY-MUSIC, from hip-hop to soul, from George Clinton to War, from zydeco to soca. Its only trouble is that it's *too* broad sometimes, and likely to result in some disgruntlement among subscribers with varying tastes. Look for upcoming changes to divide this large list into more specified smaller ones.

Owner or Contact Charles L. Isabell, funky-music-request@mit.edu

To Subscribe Send a politely worded request to funky-music-request@mit.edu. To unsubscribe, send a politely worded request to funky-music-request@mit.edu. Send all articles to FUNKY-MUSIC@mit.edu.

If you sense from these listings that funk, jazz, rap, hip-hop, and blues genres are ready to explode into dozens of Websites, mailing lists, and newsgroups, with each dedicated to its own sub-category, you're right. Keep an eye out for those changes.

Hard Bop Cafe

http://www.mbnet.mb.ca/~mcgonig/

With a focus on Winnepeg Jazz, the Hard Bop Cafe is your Canadian jazz source, featuring regularly updated information about concerts, festivals, club lists, jazz radio programming, and reviews of concerts and recordings. There's a broad list of other sources as well: I liked the "Miles Davis for Beginners" link, with a short biography on the late trumpeter and extended bibliography, as well as album suggestions for the uninitiated listener. Listings in French and English.

JazzNET

http://www.dnai.com/~lmcohen/

From Pat Metheny to artists on the Blue Note and Verve record labels, JazzNET is an excellent place to begin your search for jazz on the Internet. Offering information about fan clubs, press kits, and several musical calendars, JazzNET also is a source for FTP sites and other online jazz hotspots. I particularly liked their extensive listings of club directories—including both addresses (by city) and upcoming shows at various venues.

JAZZ Online

http://www.flightpath.com/JAZZ/Default.HTML

This Internet source for jazz (see Figure 2.15) divides itself into two large categories: Traditional styles—including be-bop, big band, traditional, straight-ahead, and progressive—and contemporary, including new age and world music styles. With up-to-date information about upcoming tours, record labels, contests, new CDs, and an art gallery, Jazz Online seems an ideal source for jazz fans of all ages and preferences.

Figure 2.15:
JAZZ Online's home hage welcomes you with a great image of Louis Armstrong.

This site may be under reconstruction: After months of easy access, it's hard to reach lately. Keep trying, though; it's worth the trouble.

WNUR-FM JazzWeb Server

http://www.acns.nwu.edu/jazz/

A source for all things jazzish, including its retailers on the Net, labels, jazz improv courses, history, FAQs, radio stations' online sites, and biographical material, WNUR also features archives of the rec.music.bluenote newsgroup discussions and two kinds of charts: Those of jazz album sales, and charts of original compositions, in files from 60-124KB. Look for this section to expand.

JAZZ, R & B, AND RAP: ARTISTS LISTINGS

Beastie Boys

alt.music.beastie-boys

http://nando.net:80/music/gm/BeastieBoys/

Ad-Rock, Mike D., and MCA, three Brooklynites (see Figure 2.16) who collaborate to form one of the most successful rap acts in the world, have their own newsgroup as well as their own WWW page. Listings feature current release, T-shirt, and tour info, and numerous discussions devoted to the trio's best lines.

http://nando.net/music/gm/ features myriad other rising rap and hip-hop stars: Check out their "Music Kitchen" stop (see Figure 2.17) for more info.

Blues Brothers

alt.fan.blues-brothers

Though nearly fifteen years have elapsed since their final tour and recording, John Belushi and Dan Aykroyd's hot blues band still lives on the Internet.

Figure 2.16:
Ad-Rock, Mike D., and MCA: The Beastie Boys.
More rhymes than Jamaica got mangoes.

Blues Traveler

alt.music.blues-traveler

Blues Traveler is one of the few full-fledged blues acts who've taken their fan clubs to the Net—right now. Wait a few months, and I'll bet you'll find dozens more.

Miles Davis

MILES

One of "the single most influential [people] in all of modern jazz," Davis provided us with music that will affect generations of musicians. This list is devoted entirely to the shy trumpeter and discussions of the influence his music has on

Figure 2.17:
nando.net's "Music Kitchen" invites you to sit down and enjoy some tasty musical bites.

the direction of jazz. With a perfect mixed focus on the past, present, and future of the genre, I found MILES one of the most well-balanced mailers on the Net.

Keywords Miles Davis, jazz, music, discussion

Owner or Contact Tom Buck, TBUCK@KNOX.BITNET

To Subscribe E-mail to LISTSERV@HEARN.NIC.SURFNET.NL; in the body of the message type **SUBSCRIBE MILES** followed by your full name. To unsubscribe, send the **UNSUB MILES** command in e-mail to LISTSERV@HEARN.NIC.SURFNET.NL. Send all other list-related commands to LISTSERV@HEARN.NIC.SURFNET.NL; send **HELP** for a list of available commands. Send articles to MILES@HEARN. NIC.SURFNET.NL.

John Hiatt

SHOT-OF-RHYTHM

http://www.unicom.com/1/john-hiatt

Bluesman and songwriter Hiatt brushes shoulders with such musical greats as Ry Cooder, Bonnie Raitt, and Michael Ward. His fans maintain SHOT-OF-RHYTHM as a small and dedicated mailing list to discuss old recordings and current projects, including his recent *Hiatt Comes Alive at Budokan?*. Archives for the list are housed in the Website, along with promotional press, photos, and other Hiatt-related news.

Code U

Owner or Contact Chip Rosenthal, shot-of-rhythm-request@chinacat.unicom.com

To Subscribe E-mail shot-of-rhythm-request@chinacat.unicom.com; in the body of the message, type **SUBSCRIBE SHOT-OF-RHYTHM** followed by your real name. To unsubscribe, send the command **UNSUBSCRIBE SHOT-OF-RHYTHM** in e-mail to shot-of-rhythm-request@chinacat.unicom.com. Information on where to send articles will be provided upon subscribing.

MC 900 FT Jesus

http://american.recordings.com/American_Artists/MC_900FT_Jesus/mc_home.html

The innovative Texan rapper/jazzman has a site on American Records (see Figure 2.18), the label that released his recent *One Step Ahead of the Spider*. Lots of photos and several video clips.

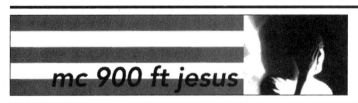

Figure 2.18:
MC 900 FT Jesus,
lurking in his Internet
site. With great music
and lyrics, he's not as
sinister as he looks.

Primus

alt.music.primus

http://iris3.carb.nist.gov:8000/pub/ram/music/primus/primus.html

You can almost always start a flamewar by posting to a fan group with the message: "[the artist whose fan group it is] Sucks!" except that at alt.music.primus, devoted to the band who closes its live show with "We're Primus and we suck!", there are already several such listings, all by supporters of this Bay Area trio. Fans of Primus' twisted funk are looking for bootleg recordings, e-mail addresses for members of the band, and the normal T-shirt/sticker paraphernalia. Primus sucks!...and they have a great newsgroup, too.

Like their music, Primus' Website is extremely funky and unpredictable; Occasionally, I had trouble accessing it.

Run-DMC

alt.fan.run-dmc

Few rap and hip-hop artists currently have fan groups on the Net, but these originators of old-school style maintain a well-subscribed Net connection.

It happens very rarely, but I've come across some systems that cannot access alt.fan.run-dmc *or* alt.music.primus. *Considering both groups' popularity, that's ridiculous: If you discover a particular newsgroup you cannot access, and have reason to believe it's because your particular network isn't connected to it, feel free to contact your system administrator to find out why.*

Stevie Ray Vaughan

http://www.quadralay.com/www/Austin/AustinMusic/srv/StevieRayVaughan.html

The Quadralay corporation's Austin guide is a great source for music, including a Web page for the late bluesman Stevie Ray Vaughan. Includes many excellent photos (see Figure 2.19), history, and discographies.

Figure 2.19:
Several images of the legendary Stevie Ray Vaughan, downloaded from his Web page

Rock and Pop Music

Here's the monster: The Internet's fastest-growing musical category, Rock and Pop marks the spot where commercial artists and the exploding music industry meet this hot new multimedium. It's where you'll find the major acts, the MTV stars, the current big guns of "alternative" radio: From AC/DC to ZZ Top, from kings Elvis Costello and Elvis Presley to Queen and Prince, this is the stop for Rock and Pop.

Hey, I sorta like that....

One thing to remember about this category is that it's not just filled with mega-artists: Besides R.E.M. and U2, you'll also discover in-depth profiles for such relative unknowns as Guided By Voices, the MC5, or the Grifters among Rock and Pop's mailing lists, newsgroups, and Websites. Don't limit yourself to just your favorite artists in this category: Look around.

ROCK AND POP: GENERAL LISTINGS

Addicted to Noise Online Magazine

http://www.addict.com/ATN/

See "Calendars and Magazines."

If you're looking for starting places in this section, you might try alt.music.misc.*, though it appears to be a huge and ungainly newsgroup, it is still a good bet. Just spend some time getting to know your way around, and then zero in on particular artists—or their Websites, lists, or newsgroups—that interest you.*

General Music

alt.music
bit.listserv.allmusic

Though alt.music lacks a focus, it does host a wide range of listings, from Billy Idol to Bob Marley. This first generic nerwsgroup is good, though, if you're just puttering. The listserv group offers a mishmash of styles, too, from PJ Harvey to the Beach Boys to the Beatles. If you want allmusic, you've got allmusic....

Having trouble finding a particular newsgroup? Don't forget that with over 12,000 newsgroups on the Internet, all service providers cannot possibly connect to all of them. If you want to cast a vote for one you can't reach, contact your provider's system administrator.

General Rock & Roll

alt.rock-roll
alt.rock-roll.classic
alt.rock-roll.hard

I can't begin to differentiate among these three except to say that album-oriented radio rock from the late 1970s seems to dominate. If a certain kind of music pounds out of an eight-cylinder car on Main Street somewhere in America's heartland, however, you'll probably find it talked about on one of these three newsgroups.

Grunge Rock

GRUNGE-L

The term *grunge*, an unfortunate catch-all marketing slogan for 1990s rock, casts a dripping umbrella over more music than its original purveyors—discordant, muddy punk rock acts, some of whom appeared on Seattle's Sub Pop record label—intended. This list makes careful note that its musical focus isn't just on Seattle or Sub Pop (see Figure 2.20), but on all topics related to the form. Too much Pearl Jam for my taste, but a well-honed and coherent list nonetheless.

Code D (For a description of these codes, see "Mailing List Codes" in "Classical Music.")

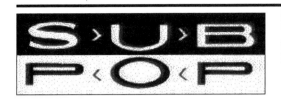

Figure 2.20:
The label that inspired a thousand grunge acts: Seattle's famous Sub Pop, found at
http://www.subpop.com/

Owner or Contact Jon Hilgren, rockin@mudhoney.micro.umn.edu

To Subscribe E-mail LISTSERV@ubvm.cc.ubvm.edu; in the body of the message, type **SUBSCRIBE GRUNGE-L** followed by your real name. To unsubscribe, send the command **UNSUBSCRIBE GRUNGE-L** in e-mail to LISTSERV@ubvm.cc.ubvm.edu. Send all other list-related commands to LISTSERV@ubvm.cc.ubvm.edu. For assistance, send the command **HELP**. Send all articles to GRUNGE-L@ubvm.cc.ubvm.edu.

Guitar Tabulature Archives

ftp.nevada.edu

If you're looking for guitar chord listings to your favorite artists' songs, try this site. Like the lyrics archive sunet.se that appears later in this section, however, the tabulature archive is very busy most of the time.

You can find many artists' lyrics and tabulature—if such files exist—available on their Websites.

Heavy Metal Rock

alt.rock-roll.metal
alt.rock-roll.metal.heavy
alt.rock-roll.metal.death

Like the rock-roll newsgroups, the different metal groups seem to favor similar rosters, with Metallica, Slayer, and Anthrax leading the fray. alt.rock-roll.metal.death also dips into the grindcore genre (see "Alternative Music"), a molten blend of punk and metal delivered at lightning speed, with bands including Godflesh and Napalm Death. Smile and have a nice day.

Lyrics Archives

ftp.sunet.se

This lyrical one-stop purports to provide the words to your favorite songs, but has become so popular that I can rarely access it.

Miscellaneous Rock and Pop Music

alt.music.misc

Some newsgroups suffer by just being a garage sale of a particular subject, and that's how it feels here: Discussions are all over the place, from listings selling baritone horns and tubas to discussions on artists as diverse as Steve Perry, Pearl Jam, ELP, the Cure, Indigo Girls, and the Pixies. The most interesting info was Net-oriented: A lengthy discussion of IUMA's download site (see "Alternative Music" for their URL), announcements and press releases for on-line music magazines, and a promotion for VirtualRadio (also listed in "Alternative Music"). If you like flea markets, you'll enjoy just perusing the myriad listings from this group, and you can tune in tomorrow for a whole new batch.

"Music Lovers"

rec.music.misc

The self-described "Music Lovers" group is another awesomely diverse, large, and generic stop with a zillion listings, whose fans—of artists from Elton John to Meat Puppets—compete for space. The word at rec.music.misc, however, is *mainstream*; including plenty of U.S. and British Top 40 charts, bio material, and tour/concert/release info for the Net-head not into the alternative scene.

Oldies Rock

alt.rock-roll.oldies

Oldies are hard to define, but greased-back rockers such as Buddy and Elvis and Carl get most of the mentions here, with plenty of catalogues and rare 45s for sale.

If you're a record collector, don't forget to check out the "Special Collectors' Section" later in this part.

Online Music Database

http://www.cecer.army.mil/urnett/MDB/

Here's a good general music directory to search for info on your favorite artist by name, album, track, style, language, or country of origin. This site is a rock encyclopedia, a growing resource that, though centered in mainstream listening, is certain to improve with increased usage. Curiously, I found many older bands I liked, but fewer listings for more current bands the same members were in. Stop by occasionally to see how increased data will better hone this database.

You can also search this database's artist listings by the person who submitted their original descriptions. Once you discover someone who has similar tastes, you'll have found a reliable tool for recommendation.

Progressive Music

alt.music.progressive

Like an alt.exotic-music gone amok, the huge "progressive" newsgroup suffers from too broad a definition of genre: That I found discussions for Yes, ELP, Kansas, Genesis, Asia, Roxy Music, and Dead Can Dance all listed in its directory gives you some indication of its focus—there ain't one. Interesting, but plainly a flea-market stop. I couldn't differentiate between this newsgroup and alt.rock-roll.progressive; both seemed to be generic groups strictly for browsing.

Progressive Rock

alt.rock-roll.progressive

Uh...*progressive* seems to be in the eye—or ear—of the progressor, because this forum is all over the map. Lots of late-70s and 80s supergroups, and some fusion jazz. Another argument for clearly focused newsgroups.

RockWeb Interactive

http://www.rock.net/

RockWeb Interactive (see Figure 2.21) is a less-than-focused site that changes every time I access it: Currently, it's offering information about a few major artists including Spin Doctors, Blues Traveler, God Street Wine, and Black Crowes. It also houses some lesser-known artists, such as Gila Monsters, Zero, and Zoo People. RWI once offered an excellent head-banging "Concrete Forum," where you could find info about such "Hard Music" artists as Big Chief, Extreme, Megadeth, and Machine Head, but it seems to have been replaced with a massive—and pretty dull—newsletter archive. Not sure what to expect from them in the future.

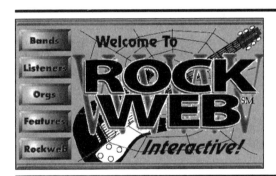

Figure 2.21:
RockWeb Interactive seems to be in a state of flux, but ushers you into its current version with this Welcome screen.

Syntho-Pop Music

alt.music.synthpop

Remember when music videos were born? Heavily fortified with artists including Howard Jones, OMD, Tears for Fears, Pet Shop Boys, Alphaville, Gary Numan, and Ultravox, this group seems to be a hangout for devotees of the early-1980s synthesizer pop that featured on MTV's first playlists. It's not all old, however: About every fifth listing is something on Depeche Mode, one of very few artists in the genre that survived into the 1990s.

I'd better not say whether I feel DM's survival is a good thing....

U.K. Pop Music

http://www.elmail.co.uk/music/MusicBase

Proof: With artists like Creation, Radiohead, Human League, PWEI, and Stone Roses first on its roster, you know it's a U.K.-only thang, and a very mainstream pop stop at that.

ROCK AND POP: ARTIST LISTINGS

AC/DC

alt.rock-roll.acdc

I'm on the information super-Highway to Hell....

Alice Cooper

SICKTHINGS

He's weird, he's disgusting, he had a cameo in *Wayne's World*. He also has a twisted mailing list for his fans on the Internet.

Code U (For a description of these codes, see "Mailing List Codes" in "Classical Music.")

Owner or Contact Hunter Goatley, goathunter@wkuvx1.wku.edu

To Subscribe E-mail MXserver@wkuvx1.wku.edu; in the body of the message, type **SUBSCRIBE SICKTHINGS** followed by your real name. To unsubscribe, send the command **UNSUB SICKTHINGS** in e-mail to MXserver@wkuvx1.wku.edu. Send all other list-related commands to MXserver@wkuvx1.wku.edu. Send all articles to SICKTHINGS@wkuvx1.wku.edu.

Bad Religion

http://nebuleuse.enst-bretagne.fr/~lepoulti/BAD.RELIGION/

Justice is served: A very new, rather rickety site for the longtime punk band who, oddly enough, have received their due because of the hype behind artists such as Green Day and Rancid—who weren't even born when Bad Religion were making their first records.

Beatles

rec.music.beatles

So there were these four guys, right? And one day they said: "Hey, let's start a band!" And one of them said, "but we need haircuts first…."

http://turtle.ncsa.uiuc.edu/alan/beatles.html

The Beatles' Website features megabytes of lyrics and images dedicated to the Fab Four, and includes a list of all 87 figures found on the cover of *Sgt. Pepper*. Other topics of interest include the "Paul is Dead" myth and "The Beatles meet the Simpsons." Check out the links to Britannica Online and additional Beatles Web pages.

The Sorcerer's Apprentice

It's a myth that computers are only as smart as those who program them; they're just more stubborn. One potential glitch worth mentioning is that of the unmoderated mailing list that, combined with a computer that can't recognize an UNSUBSCRIBE command, can deliver far more information to your e-mailbox than you could ever read, like Mickey Mouse's helpful broom and bucket under their spell in *Fantasia*.

A fellow newbie subscribed to an unnamed, unmoderated fan group list and began receiving posts…*lots* of posts. Her Internet service provider charged for e-mail by the piece, and she quickly recognized an expensive venture not worth the cost.

She tried to unsubscribe but the computerized list manager, through some error or another, didn't recognize her request and continued to ship posts, more daunting now, to her e-mailbox. She tried to cancel again from a work computer, but accidentally assigned herself another subscription—to her work address. Now she had two subscriptions to a list she didn't want: Get the idea of the potential troubles?

Björk

http://math-www.uio.no/bjork/index.html

Don't let the first screens—whose text appears in Norwegian—scare you off: This site is a simple and easily navigated stop that includes a discography, several interviews, and articles on the ex-Sugarcubes' lead singer, who's embarked on a solo career. You can also order her music and get other mailing-list addresses. Frequent use of the ø key.

Because they're so wildly creative, I recommend the following entries as good starting places for this section. You may not be into Jimmy Buffett's music, but his Website is an excellent example of the Internet's most creative—and, for its subject, most complete—musical resources.

Jimmy Buffett

BUFFETT

For twenty years, Jimmy Buffett has been making Caribbean-leaning country rock/party music for his "parrothead" fans, who spend their time at this site trading info on news of his records, books, and upcoming and recent tours.

Then she went on vacation for two weeks.

Digital information takes up so little physical space, we tend to forget about it. But when my friend returned home, she had accumulated over a thousand pieces of e-mail that—because of her mail program's limitations—she would have to open one-by-one in order to delete, with more posts headed her way. And she hadn't yet gone to work.

"I actually considered selling my computer right then and there and buying another one," she says. "I wondered if I could just tell my service provider that I'd died and wanted to close out that mailbox."

But she called an acquaintance, a patron saint of computer networkings, who assuaged her fears and, within a couple of days, helped her override her mailing program, cancel her subscription, and apply for credit for her e-mail charges.

"I was scared at first that everything was irreversible," she says. "But I realize now you just have to think and command like a machine in order to get your human needs met. You just need to persevere with the simple things you know you're doing right." She subscribes now to moderated lists in digest form, and has no more dreams of marching brooms bringing buckets of mail.

Keywords: music, Buffett, Parrothead, Jimmy Buffett

Owner or Contact Bill Lack, Lack_William_E1@msmail.muohio.edu

To Subscribe E-mail LISTSERV@miamiu.acs.muohio.edu; in the body of the message, type **SUBSCRIBE BUFFETT** followed by your real name. To unsubscribe, send the command **UNSUB BUFFETT** in e-mail to LISTSERV@miamiu.acs.muohio. edu. Send all other list-related commands to LISTSERV@miamiu.acs.muohio.edu. Send all articles to BUFFETT@miamiu.acs.muohio.edu.

alt.fan.jimmy-buffett

Some subscribers may also be able to access alt.fan.jimmy-buffet, *another forum with a different spelling. "Buffett" is the correct spelling of Jimmy's name.*

http://ameritech.ils.nwu.edu/buffett/buffett.html

Buffett's newsgroups are a fan's paradise, with no tale too tawdry to tell about a favorite show, story, or song. At the Website (see Figure 2.22), check out the "Coconut Modem, AOL's only Parrothead publication;" learn about Pirates and about how to help save manatees; pop into the "CocoNet Boat Bar" for Boat Drinks, and quite possibly the only alcoholic Jell-O recipes on

Figure 2.22:
Sometimes you forget that you're actually looking for Jimmy Buffett at his partycentric Website.

the Internet. Oh, wait—you're a Buffett fan, too? Plenty of lyrics, FAQs, tour dates, guitar chords, images, and sounds to go with all this partyphernalia.

Kate Bush

rec.music.gaffa

See listing in "Alternative Music."

Cocteau Twins

http://garnet.berkeley.edu:8080/cocteau.html

A simple but well-maintaned Web page featuring news and rumors about the Cocteau Twins, including its members, history, and lyrics. The site includes a huge gallery of downloadable pictures, graphics, and artwork, as well as video clips and sound files, and an e-mail form for fans to address the band directly.

Elvis Costello

COSTELLO

Remarkably prolific Costello continues to write interesting music, and his mailing list is dedicated to his musical history, lyrics, and personal trivia, as well as upcoming appearances and recent collaborations with other musicians, such as the Kronos String Quartet. This newsgroup sounds smart and literate, just like Elvis.

Code D

Owner or Contact Danny Hernandez, djh@gnu.ai.mit.edu

To Subscribe Send a politely worded request to costello-request@gnu.ai.mit.edu. To unsubscribe, send a politely worded request to costello-request@gnu.ai.mit.edu. Send all articles to COSTELLO@gnu.ai.mit.edu.

http://east.isx.com/~schnitzi/elvis.html

Elvis' Website (see Figure 2.23) contains a good "What's New?" section with dated entries, mailing list, FAQs, guitar tabulature to some of his more famous songs, and reviews and reports of upcoming events.

Figure 2.23:
Elvis Costello may look happy, but is he really? Find out at his Website.

Cranberries

http://www.nada.kth.se/~d90-fgi/Cranberries/cranberries.html

The "Official Unofficial" home page is pretty rough, evidently translated from the Swedish, with more disclaimers and warnings than actual text or images… *one*, that I could find.

Counting Crows

http://hammers.wwa.com/hammers/crows/discog.html

Currently, a discography-only site for this Grammy-nominated band.

Depeche Mode

http://www.cis.ufl.edu/~sag/dm/

Reach out, click mouse... Oops, sorry: FAQs, lyric sheets, discography, GIFs, and a zillion other FTP, Gopher, and WWW-related sites for this band. Is it true DM's name actually means *peach of the day*?

Danzig

alt.music.danzig

See listing in "Alternative Music."

Enigma

http://www.hsr.no/~joarg/Enigma.html

Up-to-date info on Michael Cretu and the upcoming Enigma *Three*, with illustrated discographies, lyrics, articles, and recommendations for "Enigma-like" music. The large picture gallery features over 35 images—with occasional glitches in downloading.

Enya

alt.music.enya

See listing in "International and Ethnic Music."

Peter Gabriel

alt.music.peter-gabriel

http://www.cs.clemson.edu/~junderw/pg.html

The ex-Genesis member, ur-MTV icon, and WOMAD music festival promoter continues to fill the music scene with occasional film-soundtrack work

(*Natural Born Killers* and *Philadelphia*) when he's not writing great pop songs. The Website *And Through The Wire* contains, oddly, a big classifieds section, as well as discographies, FAQs, interviews and reviews, biography, plus an address for WOMAD online. You'll also find links to eight other home pages, including Genesis'. Home-made and user-friendly.

 If you're a fan of Phil Collins, you'll find him bashed repeatedly in the alt.music. peter-gabriel *newsgroup. Sorry.*

Grateful Dead

DEAD-HEADS

DEAD-HEADS' one-paragraph description makes it sound as if the site is geared more toward high-strung businessmen than the sleepy, peace-loving Dead-heads I know: "Our goal is to allow busy people to stay in touch with timely ticket information, set lists, and miscellaneous info about the Grateful Dead. Discussion, questions, and long rambling reviews are not welcome here."

Wow…what would Jerry say to that, man?

Code M

Owner or Contact DEAD-HEADS-Approval@gdead.berkeley.edu

To Subscribe E-mail Majordomo@gdead.berkeley.edu; in the body of the message, type **SUBSCRIBE DEAD-HEADS**. To unsubscribe, send e-mail to Majordomo@gdead. berkeley.edu; in the body of the message, type **UNSUBSCRIBE DEAD-HEADS**. Send all other list-related commands to Majordomo@gdead.berkeley.edu. For assistance, send the command **HELP**. Send all articles to DEAD-HEADS@gdead.berkeley.edu.

DEAD-FLAMES

Echoed to the USENET newsgroup, rec.music.gdead, this site might be more the true Deadhead's style: Mellow, easy-going, and utterly Dead-icated. Also see the DAT-Heads Website in "Special Collectors' Section."

Code D

Owner or Contact Eric J. Simon, dead-flames-approval@gdead.berkeley.edu

To Subscribe E-mail Majordomo@gdead.berkeley.edu; in the body of the message, type **SUBSCRIBE DEAD-FLAMES**. To unsubscribe, e-mail Majordomo@

gdead.berkeley.edu; in the body of the message, type **UNSUBSCRIBE DEAD-FLAMES**. Send all other list-related commands to Majordomo@gdead.berkeley.edu. For assistance, send the command **HELP**. Send all articles to DEAD-FLAMES@gdead.berkeley.edu.

rec.music.gdead

Though they've been around for more than twenty years now, the Grateful Dead continue to draw new fans—and old ones who just bought a modem—to their newsgroup.

I could never successfully access any given URLs for Grateful Dead Websites, or I'd have included those, too.

Green Day

http://www.cs.caltech.edu/~adam/greenday.html

Being obnoxious got Green Day (see Figure 2.24) where they are now: The green-haired Grammy-winning Bay Area trio, whose best-selling *Dookie* broke every sales expectation last year, are the band of the minute. This site's "Other Recommended Bands" section is a great punk primer, with dozens of links to other fine bands. I like the link entitled "If You Like Green Day, Flame The Losers Who Don't," which takes you to http://cybersight.com/cgi-bin/cs/newsic/news/.92, a Green Day hate-mail hub. Hey, equal time, dudes.

Figure 2.24:
Call a pop album Dookie, sell a zillion copies. Green Day's Website features cover art and an excellent punk primer.

Jimi Hendrix

HEY-JOE

The Seattle guitar-master died young, but his music lives on for yet another generation of fans, this time on the Internet.

Code D

Owner or Contact Joel Abbott, abbott@ms.uky.edu

To Subscribe E-mail hey-joe-request@ms.uky.edu; in the subject of the message, type **SUBSCRIBE**. To unsubscribe, send the command **UNSUBSCRIBE** in the subject line of an e-mail to hey-joe-request@ms.uky.edu. Send all articles to HEY-JOE@ms.uky.edu.

Jane's Addiction

JANES-ADDICTION

The band no longer exists, but founder Perry Farrell's other projects—Porno For Pyros and the smash Lollapalooza summer festivals—also get discussed here.

Code D

Owner or Contact Joel Abbott, abbott@ms.uky.edu

To Subscribe E-mail janes-addiction-request@ms.uky.edu; in the subject of the message, type **SUBSCRIBE**. To unsubscribe, send the command **UNSUBSCRIBE** in the subject of an e-mail to janes-addiction-request@ms.uky.edu. Send all articles to JANES-ADDICTION@ms.uky.edu.

http://raptor.sccs.swarthmore.edu/jahall/dox/JA.html

The Jane's Addiction Website contains plenty of sounds, downloadable pictures, biographies, and an FTP site listing.

Led Zeppelin

alt.music.led-zeppelin

With ex-Zep John Paul Jones on a comeback tour with alternative-opera diva Diamanda Galas, and Jimmy Page and Robert Plant recently hanging out together again, this mega-fan group is sure to get bigger. If you are a Led Zep fan, you may also enjoy the upcoming section "When Dinosaurs Ruled the Earth."

Madonna

alt.fan.madonna

You didn't expect the reigning pop queen of reinvention to miss another chance for exposing herself, did you? As a subscriber to this list, you can expect posts on every conceivable Madonna-centered subject.

When Dinosaurs Ruled the Earth

Here are a few URLs that will direct you to Websites for the BIG ROCK ACTS that figured so prominently in the 1970s:

- ◆ Aerosmith: http://coos.dartmouth.edu/~jeoh/

- ◆ Deep Purple: http://www.tecc.co.uk/public/purple/Purple.html

- ◆ Emerson, Lake and Palmer: http://bliss.berkeley.edu/elp/

- ◆ Iron Maiden: http://www.cs.tufts.edu/~stratton/maiden/maiden.html

- ◆ Billy Joel: http://www.usacs.rutgers.edu/~rotton/bjoel.html

- ◆ Kiss: http://www.galcit.caltech.edu/~aure/strwys.html

- ◆ Led Zeppelin: http://uvacs.cs.virginia.edu/~jsw2y/zeppelin/zeppelin.html

- ◆ Rush: http://www.cerf.net/~jlang/rushfan.html

- ◆ Toto: http://www.helsinki.fi/~jhaakana/toto/toto.html

- ◆ Van Halen: http://fallon.com/mattj/vh/vhpage.html

- ◆ Yes: http://www.cen.uiuc.edu/~eal10735/yes.html

Rawwwk, dude.

Marillion

alt.music.marillion

Lots of Net hype behind this Canadian band, and a former leader/court jester named Fish.

Metallica

alt.rock-roll.metal.metallica

http://freeabel.geom.umn.edu:8000/metallica/metallica.html

I'm not a heavy metal fan *per se*, but these Bay Area arena-masters are smart and sophisticated musicians and evidently nice guys as well. And "Enter Sandman" *is* a great song. The newsgroup is loaded with adolescent gushing (and a few other Metallica-related URLs that seem to be springing up), while the Website contains just what you'd expect: Lyrics, digitized songs, and a good written history of the band. Now excuse me while I go grow my hair.

Midnight Oil

POWDERWORKS

Loudly political, hugely popular in their homeland of Australia as well as in the U.S., Midnight Oil maintains a popular mailing list featuring discussion of upcoming tours and releases and whereabouts of towering lead singer and sometime Aussie-senate candidate Peter Garrett.

Code M

Owner or Contact Tim Hunter, tim@boulder.colorado.edu, Brian Perry, perry@bng.ge.com

To Subscribe E-mail to Majordomo@cs.colorado.edu; in the body of the message, type **SUBSCRIBE POWDERWORKS**. To unsubscribe, send e-mail to Majordomo@cs.colorado.edu; in the body of the message, type **UNSUBSCRIBE POWDERWORKS**. Send all other list-related commands to Majordomo@cs. colorado.edu. For assistance, send the command **HELP**. Send all articles to POWDERWORKS @cs. colorado.edu.

Nine Inch Nails

alt.music.nin

http://www.scri.fsu.edu/~patters/nin.html

NIN's Newsgroup listing appears in the "Alternative Music" section, of course, but the band is huge now, appealing to a larger audience than they've ever imagined. With one request for it coming every 25 seconds, the Web page (see Figure 2.25) is quite complete: You can see and hear plenty of music, read lyrics, and check out "NINformation on the NINternet": The band's discography, FAQ, tour info, guitar tabulature, reviews, and other WWW links. Cool; maybe it'll cheer Trent up.

Figure 2.25:
One of several computer-inspired Nine Inch Nails logos from their Web page

Nirvana

http://www2.ecst.csuchico.edu/~jedi/nirvana.html

Speaking of mega-groups, Nirvana's Web page, Verse Chorus Verse, (see Figure 2.26) is packed with FAQs, concert anthologies, the band's covers and tributes, and interviews. You can also tap into an image gallery with thumb-nailed pictures, soundbytes, and other Nirvanean resources, including links to Sub Pop and DGC record company sites and IUMA.

I have a problem, though, with this site: Kurt Cobain's suicide spoke to a generation, but it took me much searching to find the first mention of it on this web page. I think some up-front discussion on the subject—recommendations

Figure 2.26:
The late Kurt Cobain greets you at Verse Chorus Verse, Nirvana's home page on the WWW.

for preventive tactics, helpful books, hotlines, or Net-related resources, perhaps, for people in need—deserves some space here. Why not use a Website like this to educate young Net-surfers, in *addition* to highlighting the band's music?

Gary Numan

NUMAN

I don't have a clue what quirky new-waver Gary Numan ever did after his smash "Cars" single, but he has a Net following nonetheless. Unsurprisingly, this is a quiet and intimate list.

Code D

Owner or Contact Dave Datta (datta@cs.uwp.edu)

To Subscribe Send a polite message to numan-request@cs.uwp.edu asking to be added to the mailing list. Please include your real name in this mail. Send all other commands to numan-request@cs.uwp.edu. Send articles to numan@cs.uwp.edu.

Oingo Boingo

alt.fan.oingo-boingo

Remember, they're called just "Boingo" now. Also see rec.music.movies for leader Danny Elfman's film work.

http://rhino.harvard.edu/dan/boingo/boingo.html

I couldn't access Boingo's FTP address, but did find a FAQ, discography, track listings, and song lyrics on this Website. There's a great section on Elfman himself (with his *New Yorker* caricature and an interview from America Online), revealing his upcoming plans for new movie soundtracks and more work with his band.

Pearl Jam

alt.music.pearl-jam

Mainstream grunge is big and getting bigger, as this hugely busy newsgroup proves.

http://www.skypoint.com/members/calebl/gos.html

Pearl-Jammy images, audio clips, articles, guitar tabulature, and current news about the band.

Phish

rec.music.phish

I have no proof that Grateful Dead fans are automatically subscribed to rec.music.phish, but it sure seems that way.

Pink Floyd

ECHOES

Keep your RAM open: "...a nice, civilized, and relatively quiet group of about 800 addresses that generates between 40K and 125K a day as we discuss most anything Floydian."

Code D

Owner or Contact H. W. Neff, echoes-request@fawnya.tcs.com

To Subscribe Send a politely worded request to echoes-request@fawnya.tcs.com. To unsubscribe, send a politely worded request to echoes-request@fawnya.tcs.com. Information on where to send articles will be provided upon subscribing.

http://humper.student.princeton.edu:80/floyd/

The Website is very complete with GIFs, cover art (see Figure 2.27), discography, lyrics, .AU-formatted songs, and MPEG files *The Wall*.

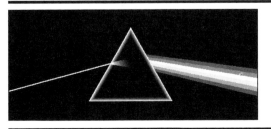

Figure 2.27:
The famous cover art from Dark Side of the Moon, Pink Floyd's best-selling album. Glad you have a color monitor?

Server Error: <Connection Refused>

L et's talk for a moment about how the WWW works: The Internet is an exponentially growing medium whose technology races to keep up with the demands of its users. For that reason, you may occasionally experience frustration logging in to a particular site.

For example, I've had repeated difficulties accessing http://www.music.sony.com; the Website for Sony Music, a major-label, big-bucks-backed URL that houses many great acts. Two of my favorite artists, former fIREHOSE bassist Mike Watt (http://www.music.sony.com/Music/ArtistInfo/Watt/) and ex-Hüsker Dü frontman Bob Mould's Sugar (http://www.music.sony.com/Music/ArtistInfo/Sugar/) have Websites inside.

I could only access Sony's site occasionally—and when I did, it moved v-e-r-y s-l-o-o-o-w-l-y. Once inside, I kept getting delivered to unfound files and to pages that denied me access. I don't know where the problems lay: Was my browser at fault? Were the phone lines crowded those days? Did the Sony site have its own glitches?

The truth is, of course, that there is no way to know. What the Net-surfer must recognize is that this remarkable medium is still in its beginning stages: Reliability and speed are still varying factors; connection problems will occasionally pop up, and the best tactic is patience and perseverance. It's worth trying, and trying, and then trying again.

One final note: The bigger the Website, the more likely it is to have high traffic. Remember this when seeking out fan groups or major record companies' sites.

Poi Dog Pondering

POI-POUNDERS

See listing in "Alternative Music."

Police

alt.music.the.police

I couldn't find an alt.fan group for Sting, nor would his Web page ever boot up. Devotees of his old band will still enjoy the many listings here, however.

Elvis Presley

http://sunsite.unc.edu/elvis/

Back after copyright challenges from the Presley estate, the Elvis home page is a friendly, funny, hospitable—and respectful—tribute to the late king of rock and roll. Most famous on this site, of course, is Andrea Burman and Philip Greenspun's incredible Tour of Graceland, complete with photos of the glitzy mansion, memorabilia, and tourists themselves. But look deeper to find a magnificent array of Elvis-related tchotchkes: Internet Elvis sightings, Elvis software, souvenirs to buy, pen-pals to write, and directions for ordering the all-important Elvis decoder ring.

Primus

PRIMUS

alt.music.primus

See listing in "Alternative Music."

Queen

alt.music.queen

The forum for Freddie Mercury's supergroup, made even more popular by the *Wayne's World* movie. Oh Mama mía, Mama mía....

Redd Kross

http://www.nando.net/music/gm/ReddKross/

A simple site for the undergound glam kings, including a discography, press clippings, and loads o' pictures.

R.E.M.

http://www.halcyon.com/rem/index.html

Remember when the B-52s were the biggest band from Athens, GA? The usual fan stuff here, focused mainly on the recent *Monster* CD, plus lyrics to older releases and pictures archived through a link to ftp.sunet.se. According to the site, the R.E.M. mailing list has shut down, but back-archives are available here, as well as links to Warner Brothers records and dozens of other related Web pages.

Rolling Stone *reports that you can get a copy of R.E.M.'s* Monster *lyrics by e-mailing* fables@lynchburg.edu *with **sendme lyrics.monster** in the message section.*

Rolling Stones

UNDERCOVER

UNDERCOVER describes itself as including "bootleg trading, how-to guitar playing advice, information about recent books, and perspectives on recent solo albums by Watts, Richards, Wood and Jagger." What Stones fan could ask for more? Echoed to the USENET newsgroup, alt.rock-roll.stones.

Code D

Owner or Contact Steve Portigal, undercover-request@tempest.cis.uoguelph.ca

To Subscribe Send a politely worded request to undercover-request@tempest.cis.uoguelph.ca. To unsubscribe, send a politely worded request to undercover-request @tempest.cis.uoguelph.ca. Information on where to send articles will be provided upon subscribing.

alt.rock-roll.stones

http://www.stones.com/

The undisputed kings of stadium rock enlisted extensive Internet coverage for their *Voodoo Lounge* tour last year. Newsgroup membership is huge and growing; expect several hundred posts to wade through. At the Website, you'll find merchandise for sale, interviews, a remarkable GIF collection, and a dozen or more interviews in massive QuickTime video clip files.

Check out the times scheduled for the re-broadcast of last year's Rolling Stones Internet multicast, the Net's first live program featuring a major musical act.

Don't miss the threads of fiction, started by fans and band members alike, that continue as members add their own fabric. In a word: Weird.

Roxy Music

http://csclub.uwaterloo.ca/u/mjklomps/roxyspage.html

Besides excellent songwriting and Bryan Ferry's remarkable voice, Roxy Music's pinup album covers have brought notoriety to this British supergroup, and here you can download GIF copies of your own. Currently, that's *all* you can do at this Website.

Todd Rundgren

alt.music.todd-rundgren

One of the first artists ever to release an interactive music project on CD-ROM, *TR-I*, Rundgren is a pioneer in the digital music scene. His small newsgroup feels like a hangout for computerheads more than fans, but maybe, in Rundgren's case, they're the same thing.

Screaming Trees

BUZZ-FACTORY

One of the better noncommercial grunge groups, Screaming Trees have a well-maintained, regularly updated list. Other pertinent subjects, such as leader Mark Lanegan's solo albums and side projects—Purple Outside, Mother Love Bone, and Solomon Grundy—get discussed as well.

Owner or Contact Greg Schmitz, gschmitz@luna.cas.usf.edu

To Subscribe E-mail LISTSERV@nosferatu.cas.usf.edu; in the body of the message, type **SUBSCRIBE BUZZ-FACTORY** followed by your real name. To unsubscribe, send the command **UNSUBSCRIBE BUZZ-FACTORY** in e-mail to LISTSERV@nosferatu.cas.usf.edu. Send all other list-related commands to LISTSERV @nosferatu.cas.usf.edu. For assistance, send the command **HELP**. Send all articles to BUZZ-FACTORY@nosferatu.cas.usf.edu.

Sisters of Mercy

http://www.cm.cf.ac.uk:/Sisters.Of.Mercy/

You can browse plenty of SOM paraphernalia here, including the usual discographies, interviews, and concert information, but I included this stop for its links to other Gothic music cultural icons, including Websites for the band Christian Death and other such pagan artists.

Slade

SLADE

British glam never dies: The often-imitated, and—fortunately—never duplicated, rock group Slade lives on, pancake makeup and all.

Owner or Contact Adri Verhoef, a3@a3.hacktic.nl, Robert Novak, rnovak@nyx.cs.du.edu

To Subscribe E-mail slade-request@gnu.ai.mit.edu; in the body of the message, type **SUBSCRIBE SLADE** followed by your e-mail address. The welcome message that you receive will indicate where to post articles. To unsubscribe, send the command **UNSUBSCRIBE** followed by your e-mail address in e-mail to slade-request@gnu.ai.mit.edu.

Smiths

smiths-fans

Though the band is no longer together, fans evidently find a substantial enough body of work to keep the list updated. Plenty of argument over

Morrissey's depressing lyrics, work by other members, and "other intellectual concerns." Hmmm.

Contact larryn@csufres.csufresno.edu

Spinal Tap

alt.fan.spinal-tap

Parody rockers from now cult-classic movie *This Is Spinal Tap*. See "Mine Goes Up to 11" in "Musicians' Resources."

Bruce Springsteen

BACKSTREETS

Grammy-award-winning Springsteen doesn't release recordings very often, but his Net fans don't care. News and lyrics, article reprints, E-Street Band members' projects, and concert tapes all keep the discussion lively.

Keywords: music, America, Springsteen

Code D

Owner or Contact Kevin Kinder, BACKSTREETS-request@virginia.edu

To Subscribe E-mail BACKSTREETS-Request@virginia.edu; in the body of the message, type **SUBSCRIBE**. To unsubscribe, send the command **UNSUBSCRIBE** in e-mail to BACKSTREETS-Request@virginia.edu. Send all other list-related commands to BACKSTREETS-Request@virginia.edu. Send all articles to BACKSTREETS@virginia.edu.

Stone Roses

http://www.musicbase.co.uk/music/sroses/rosealb.html

This recent addition coincides with the Brit band's recent *Second Coming* CD. Check out the "What's New," "Tour News," "Biographies," and "Discographies" sections.

Talking Heads

http://penguin.cc.ukans.edu/Heads/Talking_Heads.html

The Heads' is a good-sized site featuring directions to their mailing list, an in-depth FAQ file, an "All Music Guide," and discography. Since the band itself (see Figure 2.28) has been broken up for years, I was interested in the sections describing individual members' side projects.

Maybe it was the phone lines the days I tried to access this site or the browser I was using, but this URL gave me repeated loading trouble. Persevere, though, because a place like the Internet is a perfect medium for David Byrne and his fellow conspirators.

Figure 2.28:
Talking Heads:
Not the same as they
ever were

10,000 Maniacs

http://www.nd.edu/StudentLinks/mecheves/misc/10000.html

With tons o' photos and audio files courtesy of the now-defunct San Diego State sound archive, this is a friendly stop featuring graphics, lyrics, bio, and upcoming release plans. The site also includes a special section for former lead singer Natalie Merchant.

They Might Be Giants

alt.music.tmbg

See listing in "Alternative Music."

Richard Thompson

http://www.mel.dit.csiro.au/~sfy/RT/

A site evidently not too recently updated, Thompson's Web page fills you in on music he made with his wife, Linda, with other musicians, such as Fred Frith and Henry Kaiser, as well as his solo projects and pertinent live performance info. The on-site "Buried Treasures" section provides written lyrics to most— if not all?—of his songs.

U2

U2-LIST

The Irish quartet are huge, of course; so are their forums. Be prepared for thousands of postings, particularly around the release date of a new record. Their "Zoo TV" tour exploited the very media and culture on which the Internet thrives.

Code D

Owner or Contact Joel Abbott, abbott@ms.uky.edu

To Subscribe E-mail u2-list-request@ms.uky.edu; in the subject of the message, type **SUBSCRIBE**. To unsubscribe, send the command **UNSUBSCRIBE** in the subject of an e-mail to u2-list-request@ms.uky.edu. Send all articles to U2-LIST@ms.uky.edu.

alt.fan.u2
alt.music.u2

http://www2.ecst.csuchico.edu/~edge/u2.html

Both U2's newsgroups are spilling over with adoring fans and personal anecdotes, and their Web page (see Figure 2.29) offers an album-by-album breakdown of lyrics and songs (but, unfortunately, no history behind them); also interviews, b-sides, one-paragraph biographies, and a reprint of their "Interview with Negativland," which appeared in *Mondo 2000*.

Just for fun, check out http://sunsite.unc.edu/negativland/ *for the story of one artist's lengthy and ever-changing connection to U2 and American Top 40's Casey Kasem.*

Figure 2.29:
A question: Why would U2 include a fifteen-year-old picture of the band as the first you see on their Website? Just wondering.

Paul Weller/The Jam

KOSMOS

Keywords: Weller, music, UK, Britain, British

Owner or Contact Dave Lodge, DLodge@mcs.dundee.ac.uk

To Subscribe Send a politely worded request to KOSMOS-Request@mit.edu. To unsubscribe, send a politely worded request to KOSMOS-Request@mit.edu. Send all articles to KOSMOS@mit.edu.

http://biogopher.wustl.edu:70/1/audio/weller

Originally the bassist for quintessential late-70s British Mod band The Jam, Weller has since reinvented himself several times, first in the disco-poppy Style Council, and currently as a solo artist. Both his Website and mailing list reflect this last move.

XTC

CHALKHILLS

Born in the days of New Wave, British popsters XTC have two generations of followers. Discussions often include solo and members' side projects, as well as lyrics and band history. A medium-sized, well-maintained list.

Code M

Owner or Contact CHALKHILLS-Request@presto.ig.com

To Subscribe E-mail CHALKHILLS-Request@presto.ig.com; in the body of the message, type **SUBSCRIBE CHALKHILLS** followed by your e-mail address and your real name. To unsubscribe, send the command **UNSUBSCRIBE CHALKHILLS** in e-mail to CHALKHILLS-Request@presto.ig.com. Send all other list-related commands to CHALKHILLS-Request@presto.ig.com. Information on where to send articles will be supplied after subscribing.

Neil Young

http://www.uta.fi/~trkisa/hyperrust.html
http://www.iuma.com/Warner/html/Young,_Neil.html

Showing no signs of either burning out or fading away, old Young is still going strong. The first URL directs you to one fan's homegrown page, where you'll find info about Young's musicians and tours, the chronology of his many releases, collected articles, and a blurb on his nonprofit Bridge School. I liked the newsletter/chain letter section on tradeable "tape trees," in which contributors exchange favorite cassettes.

The second URL is Warner Brothers' home page for Young, which coincides with the recent release *Sleeps With Angels*. Much more slick than the first, this site provides plenty of hype, an excellent discography, and a 30-second excerpt of "Change Your Mind," the record's first single.

ZZ Top

http://www.cen.uiuc.edu/~pz3900/zztop.html

Check out the "Filezz," "Guitar Tabulaturezz," and "Picturezz" of the little ol' trio known for their Tex-Mex boogie, their beards, and their ever-so-slightly sexist videos.

ROCK AND POP: ADDITIONAL ARTISTS' MAILING LISTS

Many more pop mailing lists exist than I can include here, but I've included a sampling of others to show you the...uh...*diversity* of the bands and musicians they include. Here are some additional artists with whom you're probably already familiar.

Michael Bolton

BOLTON

...as in *boltin'* for the radio? To change the station?

Owner or Contact Beverly Woolf, woolf@pro-woolf.clark.net

To Subscribe E-mail bwoolf@pro-woolf.clark.net; in the body of the message, type **SUBSCRIBE BOLTON** followed by your e-mail address. To unsubscribe, send the command **UNSUBSCRIBE BOLTON** in e-mail to bwoolf@pro-woolf.clark.net. Information on where to send articles will be provided upon subscribing.

Dokken

BREAKING THE CHAINS

Their name means rokken—er, *rockin'*, dude....

Code M (For a description of these codes, see "Mailing List Codes" in "Classical Music.")

Owner or Contact Kirsten DeNoyelles, kirsten@mik.uky.edu

To Subscribe Send a politely worded request to kirsten@mik.uky.edu. To unsubscribe, send a politely worded request to kirsten@mik.uky.edu. Send all submissions to kirsten@mik.uky.edu.

Duran Duran

TIGER

...Simon's got a *whine*...they're pop past their *time*...and they're hungry like the wo-o-lf....

Code D

Owner or Contact Robert Novak, rnovak@acca.nmsu.edu

To Subscribe E-mail to tiger-request@acca.nmsu.edu; in the subject of the message, type **SUBSCRIBE**. The welcome message that you receive will indicate where to post articles. To unsubscribe, send the command **UNSUBSCRIBE** in the subject of an e-mail to tiger-request@acca.nmsu.edu.

Emerson, Lake & Palmer

ELP-DIGEST

Sorry, but that organ on "Roundabout" has bugged me for two decades now....

Code M

Owner or Contact John Arnold, J.Arnold@ma30.bull.com

To Subscribe Send a politely worded request to J.Arnold@ma30.bull.com. To unsubscribe, send a politely worded request to J.Arnold@ma30.bull.com. Send all submissions to J.Arnold@ma30.bull.com.

Debbie Gibson

BTL: Between the Lines

I'd love to comment, but I'm biting my tongue too hard....

Code M

Owner or Contact Myra Wong, mkwong@ucsd.edu, Felix Ng, fng@acca.nmsu.edu

To Subscribe Send a politely worded request to btl@egbt.org. To unsubscribe, send a politely worded request to btl@ebgt.org. Send all articles to btl@egbt.org.

Journey

JOURNEY-L

...featuring Steve Perry, man in eternal search of a melody.

Code U

Owner or Contact Hunter Goatley, goathunter@wkuvx1.wku.edu

To Subscribe E-mail to MXserver@wkuvx1.wku.edu; in the body of the message, type **SUBSCRIBE JOURNEY-L** followed by your real name. To unsubscribe, send the command **UNSUB JOURNEY-L** in e-mail to MXserver@wkuvx1.wku.edu. Send all other list-related commands to MXserver@wkuvx1.wku.edu. Send all articles to JOURNEY-L@wkuvx1.wku.edu.

Al Stewart

AL-STEWART

After "Year of the Cat," what?

Code D

Owner or Contact Dan Farmer, zen@fish.com

To Subscribe E-mail Majordomo@fish.com; in the body of the message, type **SUBSCRIBE AL-STEWART**. To unsubscribe, e-mail Majordomo@fish.com; in the body of the message, type **UNSUBSCRIBE AL-STEWART**. Send all other list-related commands to Majordomo@fish.com. For assistance, send the command **HELP**. Send all articles to AL-STEWART@fish.com.

Tears for Fears

TEARS4-FEARS

This band moves me, quite literally, to tears.

Code D

Owner or Contact Joel Abbott, abbott@ms.uky.edu

To Subscribe E-mail tears4-fears-request@ms.uky.edu; in the subject of the message, type **SUBSCRIBE**. To unsubscribe, send the command **UNSUBSCRIBE** in the subject of an e-mail to tears4-fears-request@ms.uky.edu. Send all articles to TEARS4-FEARS@ms.uky.edu.

ROCK AND POP: RECORD COMPANIES

Geffen Records

http://geffen.com/Guide.html

Hole, Weezer, Nirvana, Beck—the Geffen/DGC label graces many mega-acts these days; here's your chance to check out the e-versions of their bands, with the usual graphics, video, and audio files. With its link to CD*now*! (see "Special Collectors' Section" later in this part), the site makes it easy to order the discs themselves.

Warner Brothers

http://www.iuma.com/warner

See "Internet Underground Music Archive" in "Alternative Music."

International and Ethnic Music

One of my favorite sections, the International and Ethnic entries bring the sights and sounds of a global bazaar to your screen: From the sexy tangos heard in steamy Argentine dancehalls to the chilling bagpipes echoing off the Scottish moors, music from across the globe can be found on the Internet. This section also features many music genres based in ethnicity: An excellent resource for Celtic singing, for Jewish klezmer music, for Dixieland jazz and zydeco, the Internet will continue to develop as a communication tool for the world's divergent cultures, whether steeped in centuries of tradition or pursuing new trends.

Since the term *world music* often indicates a particular genre these days, please note that I use the term *international* to describe this section. What better way to begin to understand a group of people far removed from you than through their music? What better tool to use than your own computer?

INTERNATIONAL AND ETHNIC MUSIC: GENERAL LISTINGS

This section has many good starting places, but since its categories are relatively specific to the reader's tastes, I'll just offer a couple: The listing that follows, the rec.music.afro-latin *newsgroup, is an excellent one.*

Afro-Latin Music

rec.music.afro-latin

If you think Salsa is something to put on corn chips, you'll get nowhere with the group devoted to south-of-the-border musical styles, including Sambas, Rhumbas, and Bossa novas, from African/Caribbean, Brazilian,

Cuban, and Central American locales. Listings in both Spanish and English discuss artists from relatively obscure Cachao, Gilberto Gil, and Eddie Palmieri to more mainstream stars like Gloria Estefan and Ruben Blades. Also a great source for record labels and local scenes hip to Afro-Latin and other Salsa styles. ¡Sabroso!

Asian Contemporary Music

ACTMUS-L

Devoted to "serious Asian contemporary music," from current pop to historical, with listings from all over the world.

Owner or Contact Kenneth Kwan, ckkwan@acsu.buffalo.edu

To Subscribe E-mail LISTSERV@ubvm.cc.buffalo.edu; in the body of the message, type **SUBSCRIBE ACTMUS-L** followed by your real name. To unsubscribe, send the command **UNSUB ACTMUS-L** in e-mail to LISTSERV@ubvm.cc.buffalo.edu. Send all other list-related commands to LISTSERV@ubvm.cc.buffalo.edu. For assistance, send the command **HELP**. Send all articles to ACTMUS-L@ubvm.cc.buffalo.edu.

Second British Invasion

PerfectBeat

More pop than circumstance, the Second British Invasion refers here to early-80s synth pop, and features groups and musicians such as ABC, Buggles, Haircut One Hundred, and lots of early-MTV, Pop Clips, and Top of the Pops artists.

Owner or Contact Robert Novak, RNovak@nyx.cs.du.edu

To Subscribe E-mail perfect-beat-request@gnu.ai.mit.edu; in the subject of the message, type **SUBSCRIBE** followed by your e-mail address. The welcome message that you receive will indicate where to post articles. To unsubscribe, send the command **UNSUBSCRIBE** followed by your e-mail address in the subject of an e-mail to perfect-beat-request@gnu.ai.mit.edu.

Canadian Alternative Music

WESTCANALTER

"A grunge list for Western Canadian bands," WESTCANALTER is "dedicated to music which comes from Western Canada," and is proudly noncommercial in its focus.

Owner or Contact Ken Pierce, KPierce@age.cuc.ab.ca

To Subscribe E-mail LISTSERV@age.cuc.ab.ca; in the body of the message, type **SUBSCRIBE *your e-mail address* WESTCANALTER**. To unsubscribe, send the command **UNSUBSCRIBE WESTCANALTER** in e-mail to LISTSERV@age.cuc.ab.ca. Send all other list-related commands to LISTSERV@age.cuc.ab.ca. For assistance, send the command **HELP**. Send all articles to WESTCANALTER@age.cuc.ab.ca.

Celtic Music

rec.music.celtic

As good as a trip to Ireland: You can find Christy Moore, Clannad, and the Pogues' own Shane Magowan discussed at length on the Celtic Netsource. Also check out addresses for Gaelic WWWebsites, requests for Irish lullabies, and American sources for Celtic radio.

European Top 20 Chart

EURO20

This announcement-only list transmits the MTV Europe Top 20 Video chart to its subscribers—currently over 200 people—each week. Subscribers cannot post to the list.

Code M (For a description of these codes, see "Mailing List Codes" in "Classical Music.")

Owner or Contact Adri Verhoef, a3@a3.hacktic.nl, Robert Novak, RNovak@nyx.cs.du.edu

To Subscribe E-mail eu20-request@gnu.ai.mit.edu; in the subject of the message, type **SUBSCRIBE EURO20** followed by your e-mail address. To unsubscribe, send the command **UNSUBSCRIBE EURO20** followed by your e-mail address in the subject line to eu20-request@gnu.ai.mit.edu.

Finnish Classical Music

FINLANDIA

A forum for discussion about Finnish classical and modern composers, their lives and works, performing artists and orchestras, as well as Finnish publications—musical scores, books, and sheet music—and recordings in all formats.

Owner or Contact Marko Hotti, finlandia-owner@phoenix.oulu.fi

To Subscribe E-mail Majordomo@phoenix.oulu.fi; in the body of the message, type **SUBSCRIBE FINLANDIA**. To unsubscribe, send the command **UNSUBSCRIBE FINLANDIA** in e-mail to Majordomo@phoenix.oulu.fi. Send all other list-related commands to Majordomo@phoenix.oulu.fi. For assistance, send the command **HELP**. Send all articles to FINLANDIA@phoenix.oulu.fi.

French Music

alt.music.france

With thirteen messages when I checked it last, this small group is—surprise!—for Francophiles who like such artists as Patricia Kaas and Edith Piaf.

Some service providers may not be connected with the more esoteric newsgroups, alt.music.france *being one example.*

French Pop Music

CHANTER-LISTE

The first of three lists exclusively for fans of French singers and music groups. CHANTER-LISTE is the pop music list, CHANTEUR-LIST for male French singers (including Roch Voisine, Daniel Belanger, Offenbach, Les Colocs, Richard Seguin, and Vilain Pingouin), and CHANTEUSE-LIST for female singers (including Julie Masse, Axel Red, Celine Dion, France D'Amour, Marie Carmen, and

Vanessa Paradis). Members evidently also receive FAQs and announcements from sub-lists. What? No Edith Piaf?

Owner or Contact Raymond Hustad, fan-julie@musique.org

To Subscribe E-mail Majordomo@wimsey.com; in the body of the message, type **SUBSCRIBE CHANTER-LISTE**. To unsubscribe, e-mail Majordomo@wimsey.com; in the body of the message, type **UNSUBSCRIBE CHANTER-LISTE**. Send all other list-related commands to Majordomo@wimsey.com. For assistance, send the command **HELP**. Send all articles to CHANTER-LISTE@wimsey.com.

CHANTEUR-LIST

The list for fans of French male singers.

Code M

To Subscribe E-mail Majordomo@wimsey.com; in the body of the message, type **SUBSCRIBE CHANTEUR-LIST**. To unsubscribe, send e-mail to Majordomo@wimsey.com; in the body of the message, type **UNSUBSCRIBE CHANTEUR-LIST**. Send all other list-related commands to Majordomo@wimsey.com. For assistance, send the command **HELP**. Send all articles to CHANTEUR-LIST@wimsey.com.

CHANTEUSE-LIST

For fans of French female singers.

Code M

To Subscribe E-mail to Majordomo@wimsey.com; in the body of the message, type **SUBSCRIBE CHANTEUSE-LIST**. To unsubscribe, e-mail Majordomo@wimsey.com; in the body of the message, type **UNSUBSCRIBE CHANTEUSE-LIST**. Send all other list-related commands to Majordomo@wimsey.com. For assistance, send the command **HELP**. Send all articles to CHANTEUSE-LIST@wimsey.com.

It's come to my attention that these lists may include artists who simply sing in French but may not be French. I'm not enough of a French music fan to know.

German Music

de.rec.music.misc
de.rec.club.misc

de is the Internet abbreviation for Deutschland, so unless you read and type fluent German, you'll be lost in these. A representative listing: *Ja, ich vergeb' Dir, Bryan!*

Indian Music

rec.music.indian.classical

Spiced with just the slightest hint of curry, the "Hindustani and Carnatic Indian Classical Music" stop features listings for "male tanpura, made in Miraj" alongside fan info on Ravi Shankar and Ali Akbar Khan; instruments discussed include the sitar and tabla. You'll also find pertinent listings for Indian dance, concert dates, and an electronic version of *Sangeet* magazine. All in English, rec.music.indian.classical's cultural discussions are fascinating: Learn the difference between the Nattai, Gowla, Arabhi, Varali, and Sree.

rec.music.indian.misc

With more listings in Hindi, rec.music.indian.misc focuses even more on Indian culture and its music. Discussion and interpretation of lyrics, as well as musical connection to movies, send this newsgroup even further into the Indian genre. Just what *is* techno-bhangra, anyway?

Irish Music

IRTRAD-L

An excellent source for traditional Irish music, popular in both the U.K. and U.S.

To Subscribe E-mail LISTSERV@IRLEARN.BITNET; in the body of the message, type **SUB IRTRAD-L** followed by your full name.

Top-Level Geographical Domains

Just as top-level domains—those suffixes .com, .gov, .edu, and the rest—indicate which type of organization is running a particular mailing address (see "Reading E-Mail Addresses," Part One), the geographical domains found in URLs point to their countries of origin. Use your knowledge of these geographical abbreviations to improve your Netiquette: If you can help it, don't crowd a foreign site FTPing an audio file in the middle of its business day.

Following is a current list of top-level geographical domains for those countries on the Internet.

at	Austria	de	Germany	no	Norway
ca	Canada	is	Iceland	es	Spain
cl	Chile	it	Italy	se	Sweden
dk	Denmark	jp	Japan	tw	Taiwan
ec	Ecuador	kr	Korea	uk	U.K. and Ireland
fi	Finland	nz	New Zealand	us	United States
fr	France				

More of these are definitely on the way.

It's important to note that not every URL includes a geographical domain; in fact, most U.S. sites don't. Occasionally you'll discover an archaic *state* domain: one of the Internet's original conferencing sites, for example, the WELL—well.sf.ca.us—is in california, not canada.

Italian University Students

GENERAL

Based in Italy and with messages mainly in Italian, GENERAL encourages any subjects pertinent to an Italian university student: Music, computers, politics, movies, TV, the Internet—*tutto bene*, although plenty of American music, predominantly acid jazz, makes its way into the discussion lists.

Code U

Owner or Contact Paolo Montevecchi, montevec@csr.unibo.it

To Subscribe E-mail LISTPROC@csr.unibo.it; in the body of the message, type **SUBSCRIBE GENERAL** followed by your real name. To unsubscribe, send the command **UNSUB GENERAL** in e-mail to LISTPROC@csr.unibo.it. Send all other list-related commands to LISTPROC@csr.unibo.it. Send all articles to GENERAL@csr.unibo.it.

Jewish Music

alt.music.jewish

Klezmers to the left of me, klezmers to the right of me. . . . The Jewish music newsgroup is pretty klezmerized, but there are plenty of jazz and religious recordings, too; its artists range from Ofra Haza to Leonard Cohen. alt.music.jewish interested me with its political and historical discussion as well, closely relating Jewish music and culture.

Latin American Resources Database

http://www.music.indiana.edu/som/lamc/LatinAm_Resources.html

This is an excellent Website for researching Latin cultures—Mexican, Central American, and South American—for information about history, geography, politics, and music (see Figure 2.30).

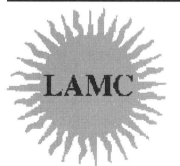

Figure 2.30:
The Latin American Music Center, found at
http://www.music.indiana.edu/som/lamc/,
is an excellent source for the sounds emanating from Mexico,
Central America, and South America.

Middle Eastern Music

Middle-Eastern Music

A long-time list for fans of the genre, an intimate and hospitable list; artists Sheila Chandra and Monsoon seem to dominate the current listings.

To Subscribe E-mail MIDDLE-EASTERN REQUEST@NIC.FUNET.FI.

New Orleans Culture

NEW-ORLEANS

Call it *Nawlins*: Not just music, but any and all aspects of the city of New Orleans, including history, politics, culture, food, restaurants, and entertainment, as well as its infamous Mardi Gras. If you subscribe, you just may smell the jambalaya and hear the brass bands coming from your PC…. And who is Thorpe and why are they all the buzz?

Code D

Owner or Contact Edward J. Branley, elendil@mintir.new-orleans.la.us

To Subscribe E-mail mail-server@mintir.new-orleans.la.us; in the body of the message, type **SUBSCRIBE NEW-ORLEANS**. To unsubscribe, send the command **UNSUBSCRIBE NEW-ORLEANS** in e-mail to mail-server@mintir.new-orleans.la.us. Send all other list-related commands to mail-server@mintir.new-orleans.la.us. For assistance, send the command **HELP**. Send all articles to NEW-ORLEANS@mintir.new-orleans.la.us.

Swedish Pop Music

alt.music.swedish-pop

To its credit, alt.music.swedish-pop isn't *entirely* focused on Abba, but Sweden's supergroup lives on in ninety percent of the newsgroup's listings. The rest of the material seems aimed at Roxette fans seeking GIFs of all styles, and other artists, such as Stina Nordenstam.

Because reggae appeals to such a broad cross-section of listeners, and because rec.music.reggae *is such a user-friendly list, I recommend it, too, as a good starting place.*

Reggae Music

rec.music.reggae

The relaxed and ebulliently positive Rastafarian newsgroup brings a remarkable culture to the Internet. The only forum of its kind for fans of roots, rockers, and dancehall reggae, it includes plenty of stops for fans of old and new artists, dates for upcoming Kingston conferences, Caribbean and U.K. reggae charts, and long, colorful tales told of the music's history. The artist who receives the most interest seems to be UB40, but Judy Mowatt, Steel Pulse, and the late Bob Marley, an old master very much alive on this stop, also fill in the postings. The reggae newsgroup seems intolerant only of flamewars.

Scottish Bagpipes

BAGPIPE

What do bagpipe players consider pressing musical topics? Why, bag seasoning, short or long practice chanters, reed care, and whether to play Highland music exactly as it's written. If these subjects are your—forgive me—bag, you'll find a closely focused and hospitable list at BAGPIPE.

Code D, M

Owner or Contact Wayne Cripps, BAGPIPE-Request@cs.dartmouth.edu

To Subscribe E-mail BAGPIPE-Request@cs.dartmouth.edu; in the subject of the message, type **SUBSCRIBE**. In your message, briefly describe your interest in the topic. To unsubscribe, send the command **UNSUBSCRIBE** in the subject of an e-mail to BAGPIPE-Request@cs.dartmouth.edu. Send all other list-related commands to BAGPIPE-Request@cs.dartmouth.edu. Send all articles to BAGPIPE@cs.dartmouth.edu.

Scottish Drumming

SIDEDRUM

Between the bagpipe and the side-drumming lists, Scots have their musical culture well represented on the Net: Questions, answers, and discussions of all things related to Scottish drumming and its music.

Code M

Owner or Contact J. J. Hayden, jj_hayden@solinet.net

To Subscribe E-mail LISTSERV@solinet.net; in the body of the message, type **SUBSCRIBE SIDEDRUM** followed by your real name. To unsubscribe, send the command **UNSUBSCRIBE SIDEDRUM** in e-mail to LISTSERV@solinet.net. Send all other list-related commands to LISTSERV@solinet.net. For assistance, send the command **HELP**. Send all articles to SIDEDRUM@solinet.net.

INTERNATIONAL AND ETHNIC MUSIC: ARTISTS LISTINGS

Abba

http://www.nvg.unit.no/moro/musikk/abba.html

I couldn't resist a stop at the international artist's site (in Norway, no less!). Well worth the connecting time.

Enya

alt.music.enya

The Irish popstress with the haunting voice has a small but rabid fan base on the Net, with postings from all over the world.

Gloria Estefan

http://nyx10.cs.du.edu:8001/~lwright/

I could never get my browser to connect me to the pop star's Web page, but here is its URL.

Julie Masse

JULIEMASSE-LISTE

One of a group of multilingual music mailing lists for fans of this rising star on the French pop music scene. Discussion in French and English.

Code M (For a description of these codes, see "Mailing List Codes" in "Classical Music.")

Owner or Contact Raymond Hustad, fan-julie@musique.org

To Subscribe E-mail Majordomo@wimsey.com; in the body of the message, type **SUBSCRIBE JULIEMASSE-LISTE**. To unsubscribe, e-mail Majordomo@wimsey.com; in the body of the message, type **UNSUBSCRIBE JULIEMASSE-LISTE**. Send all other list-related commands to Majordomo@wimsey.com. For assistance, send the command **HELP**. Send all articles to JULIEMASSE-LISTE@wimsey.com.

INTERNATIONAL AND ETHNIC MUSIC: RECORD COMPANIES

City of Tribes Communications

http://www.organic.com/Music/City.o.tribes/

A catch-all site for ZoeMagik Records and several tribal recording artists, notably Trance Mission, Lights in a Fat City, and didgeridoo player Stephen Kent (see Figure 2.31). Simple, friendly, and the music is great; another example of the possibilities of homegrown Websites.

On-U Sound Records Archives

ftp.city.ac.uk/pub/on.u.sound

This FTP site, located at City University, U.K., is home to a great independent label featuring international artists such as Dub Syndicate, Tackhead, and African Head Charge. The site includes great discographies and biographies, lyric archives, and dates for future releases. Be patient while it loads; it's worth the wait.

Figure 2.31:
Cover art for Trance Mission and Stephen Kent, both found at City of Tribes
Communications' Web page

INTERNATIONAL AND ETHNIC MUSIC: DANCE LISTINGS

Argentine Tango

TANGO

This list discusses Argentine tango events worldwide, as well as tango steps, technique, and alternative styles of the world's sexiest dancing.

Owner or Contact Shahrukh Merchant, tango-request@mitvma.mit.edu

To Subscribe E-mail LISTSERV@mitvma.mit.edu; in the body of the message, type **SUBSCRIBE TANGO** followed by your real name. To unsubscribe, send the command **UNSUBSCRIBE TANGO** in e-mail to LISTSERV@mitvma.mit.edu. Send all other list-related commands to LISTSERV@mitvma.mit.edu. For assistance, send the command **HELP**. Send all articles to TANGO@mitvma.mit.edu.

Morris Dancing

MORRIS

I wouldn't know a Morris dance from a Cotswold, a Border, a NorthWest, a Rapper, a LongSword, an Abbots Bromley, a Garland, or other English dances, but this list discusses them all, along with accompanying music and dancing traditions.

Code D (For a description of these codes, see "Mailing List Codes" in "Classical Music.")

Owner or Contact Tom Keays, libhtk@suvm.syr.edu

To Subscribe E-mail LISTSERV@suvm.acs.syr.edu; in the body of the message, type **SUBSCRIBE MORRIS** followed by your real name. To unsubscribe, send the command **UNSUBSCRIBE MORRIS** in e-mail to LISTSERV@suvm.acs.syr.edu. Send all other list-related commands to LISTSERV@suvm.acs.syr.edu. For assistance, send the command **HELP**. Send all articles to MORRIS@suvm.acs.syr.edu.

U.K. Dance Scene

UK-DANCE

With listings from both the U.K. and U.S., UK-DANCE is intended for discussion of dance music culture in the U.K.—its clubs, raves, record shops, radio, and anything else to do with the underground scene.

Contact listserv@orbital.demon.co.uk

To Subscribe Write to listserv@orbital.demon.co.uk with **subscribe uk-dance** *<Your Name>* as the first line in the message body, replacing *<Your Name>* with your real name, not your e-mail address.

Beyond Category

This section exists because there's so much great music out there that just doesn't fit into the neat compartments I've prescribed for this book. While it seems odd, at first glance, to include a mailing list for fans of barbershop-quartet singing under the same heading as an Elvis Presley seance Website or a newsgroup devoted to Dr. Demento, this list of entries only proves the wide variety of musical formats in our world, and how much music permeates our lives.

This section incorporates forums for discussing homemade musical instruments and movie soundtracks; it suggests sites where you can download files for your electronic keyboard. Like other sections in this book, it's a fun place just to browse, checking out music you may never have realized exists.

A Cappella Singing

alt.music.a-cappella
rec.music.a-cappella

One of the most clean-cut listings, alt.music.a-cappella is for singers interested in gospel, harmony singing, and unaccompanied choral music. Lots of Singers-Wanted and Singers-Looking listings, as well as warm-up exercises, suggested radio programs, a few must-have recordings, and U.K. sources for this beautiful genre. If you're into The Bobs, Take 6's, Nylons, or Knudsen Brothers, you'll appreciate the overall polite tone and earnest listings of this group. And, lest you think this all sounds too well-mannered for you, check out two ongoing rivalries—one between this group and rec.music.a-cappella, and the other between Footnotes and Tigertones, two competing groups from Princeton. Not exactly a "punk vs. hardcore" mudslinging flamewar, but hey, this is madrigal music.

In comparison to alt.music.a-cappella, the larger rec. group has more varied listings, with a focus on college listings for auditions, schools, and programs, as well as calendars of upcoming shows and events. And, of course, exhaustive back-issues of *Barbershop Digest*, all available for downloading.

Audio Binaries Database

alt.binaries.sounds.music

See listing in "Special Collectors' Section."

Barbershop Harmony

BBSHOP

The list for lovers of four-part harmonies, quartets, choruses, and the activities of organizations promoting barbershop singing, and probably the only hang-out for members of Sweet Adelines International and SPEBSQSA—the Society for the Preservation and Encouragement of Barber Shop Quartet Singing in America. Whew!

Code D (For a description of these codes, see "Mailing List Codes" in "Classical Music.")

Owner or Contact David Bowen, david.bowen@cray.com

To Subscribe Send a politely worded request to BBSHOP-Request@cray.com. In the subject line, type **SUBSCRIBE**. To unsubscribe, send a politely worded request to BBSHOP-Request@cray.com. In the subject line, type **UNSUBSCRIBE**. Send all articles to BBSHOP@cray.com.

Category Freaks

alt.music.category-freak

See description in "Alternative Music."

Chapman Stick

STICKY-FINGER

A 10- or 12- string amplified instrument with the range of a guitar but played like a piano, the Chapman Stick has a warm, harmonically rich tone. The mailing list is "open to anyone interested in the Chapman Stick, whether they play the instrument or not," and discussions include CD & tape releases, reviews, concert announcements, playing tips, equipment, teachers, and "engaging discussions between players." Sounds interesting.

Code D

Owner or Contact Dave Snowdon, dns@cs.nott.ac.uk

To Subscribe Send a politely worded request to STICKY-Request@cs.nott.ac.uk. To unsubscribe, send a politely worded request to STICKY-Request@cs.nott.ac.uk.

Choral Music

CHORALIST

A list for the choral singer interested in rehearsal techniques, composers and their works, and networking for jobs and info among college, public school, and church choral directors. Occasional discussions of choral recordings and musical editions.

Code D

Owner or Contact Patrick O'Shea, aspmo@acvax.inre.asu.edu, David Topping, asdbt@acvax.inre.asu.edu

To Subscribe E-mail LISTPROC@lists.colorado.edu; in the body of the message, type **SUBSCRIBE CHORALIST** followed by your real name. To unsubscribe, send the command **UNSUBSCRIBE CHORALIST** in e-mail to LISTPROC@lists.colorado.edu. Send all other list-related commands to LISTPROC@lists.colorado.edu. For assistance, send the command **HELP**. Send all articles to CHORALIST@lists.colorado.edu.

Christian Music

rec.music.christian

CCM means Christian Contemporary Music, and here's its source on the Net: Plenty of discussion devoted to Amy Grant, Michael W. Smith, and God, not necessarily in that order, as well as information on sacred early music. Impassioned discussions; not stuffy in the least.

Death of Rock and Roll

http://weber.u.washington.edu/~jlks/pike/DeathRR.html

Keep your hang-ups offline and your tongue firmly in cheek: A morbidly entertaining site presented in book format. You'll find chapters entitled "Famous Dates in Rock&Roll Death," and "Heroin;" a wonderfully frank Elvis Presley biography; links to such artists as John Lennon, Sid Vicious, Mama Cass, Kurt Cobain, and Marvin Gaye.

Doctor Demento and Related Music

rec.music.dementia

I first thought rec.music.dementia was devoted to music that drove people crazy, but the FAQ says it all: "The group is so named after 'The Dr. Demento Show,' a weekly radio program hosted by Barry Hansen, a/k/a Dr. Demento," its fans wallowing in "mad music and crazy comedy from out of the archives and off the wall, rare records and outrageous tapes from yesterday, today, and tomorrow." Liberal doses of Spike Jones, Al Yankovic, Stan Freeburg, and Tom Lehrer alternate with listings about Demento himself. Hmmm...maybe I was right after all....

Early Music

rec.music.early

Not the music that wakes you up in the morning, but the preclassical European sounds of the Renaissance and Baroque periods, played on lutes, recorders, and harpsichords and often sung as ballads or rounds. Various record companies (such as New Albion) and current artists (such as Ensemble Project Ars Nova) are discussed as well. The newsgroup is devoted to keeping this delightful music—and discussion of it—alive hundreds of years after it began.

Elvis Seance

http://sunsite.unc.edu/elvis/seance.html

The transcript of a seance conducted in January of 1994, in which Elvis makes clear that he hates his commemorative stamp and watches TV in heaven.

Whether or not you're an Elvis fan, you'll find it hard not to laugh out loud at The King's delightfully candid responses.

Film Music

FILMUS-L

For students and aficionados alike, this interesting list focuses both on TV and film musical recordings, from soundtracks to scores, composers, and lots of history. Although I didn't track them down, FILMUS-L promises locations and availability for research materials, and indicates possibilities for contacting film music professionals.

Code U (For a description of these codes, see "Mailing List Codes" in "Classical Music.")

Owner or Contact H. Stephen Wright, C60HSW1@NIU.BITNET, A. Ralph Papakhian, PAPAKHI@IUBVM.BITNET

To Subscribe E-mail LISTSERV@iubvm.ucs.indiana.edu; in the body of the message, type **SUBSCRIBE FILMUS-L** followed by your real name. To unsubscribe, send the command **UNSUBSCRIBE FILMUS-L** in e-mail to LISTSERV@iubvm.ucs.indiana.edu. Send all other list-related commands to LISTSERV@iubvm.ucs.indiana.edu. For assistance, send the command **HELP**. Send all articles to FILMUS-L@iubvm.ucs.indiana.edu.

Folk Song Parodies

alt.music.filk

The longtime newsgroup devoted to "songs written or enjoyed by Science Fiction fans" is undeniably one of the strangest, but in a good way: It feels a little like an elite club at first, but the writing and discussions are so imaginative you find yourself just jumping around its listings in a pleasant daze.

What kind of music is filk really? Well, "Filk is a song about futures untold/Or magic which never has been," explains the FAQ file. Uh-huh. At times sabre-edged, witty commentary; at others, like a mushroom trip at a Shakespeare festival.

Gilbert and Sullivan

SAVOYNET

If you're a Gilbert and Sullivan junkie, or just want to track down a particular tune from *Pirates of Penzance*, jack in to SAVOYNET. Everything old is new again on the Net.

Code U

Owner or Contact Ralph MacPhail Jr., R.MacPhail@cescc.bridgewater.edu

To Subscribe E-mail LISTSERV@bridgewater.edu; in the body of the message, type **SUBSCRIBE SAVOYNET** followed by your real name. To unsubscribe, send the command **UNSUB SAVOYNET** in e-mail to LISTSERV@bridgewater.edu. Send all other list-related commands to LISTSERV@bridgewater.edu. Send all articles to SAVOYNET@bridgewater.edu.

Great American Music Hall

http://www.organic.com/Music/GAMH/

As far as I could find, one of the first and only music venues accessible online: A San Francisco landmark since the 1920s, the GAMH hosts a site that (see Figure 2.32) gives you past history, ticket purchasing info, current/past/future schedules of performers—from Tom Jones to the Dog-Faced Hermans—and directions to the club from anywhere in the Bay Area. Look for many other venues to copy this service.

Figure 2.32:
At the Great American Music Hall's Web page, you can find history, schedules, and directions to the decades-old nightclub.

Guitar Tabulature

rec.music.makers.guitar.tabulature

Not a certain kind of stringed instrument, but rather listings for guitar chords to accompany your favorite songs, from Andres Segovia to Pantera, from Dire Straits' "Twisting By the Pool" to "Jesu, Joy of Man's Desiring" by some cat named Bach. See also the description for the FTP site at nevada.edu in "Rock and Pop."

K-12 Teachers' Music Instruction

k12.ed.music

k12.ed.music represents the best reason the Internet exists: That someone will use it to learn something. This group is, according to the "Welcome/Hello" file, "for discussion and questions pertaining to teaching music, dance, and drama in the educational setting, e.g., instrumental/vocal ensembles, plays, musicals, MIDI labs, dance groups, etc."

Listings offer info on everything from concert band schedules to women composers, from places to buy and repair trumpets, trombones, and violins to music theory software sources. More from "Welcome/Hello:" "Please remember that all age groups use this area, and use sensitivity when posting messages. No 'off-color' remarks are permitted." You can chew gum, though.

Karaoke Singers

alt.music.karaoke

The ever-growing popularity of this Japanese sing-along hobby may or may not be a good thing. Fans from places as divergent as Alabama and Thailand gather here to powwow, mainly about the equipment that drives their odd passion.

alt.music.karaoke *is, unfortunately, a newsgroup that some readers may find hard to access. Call (or e-mail) that system administrator!*

Lesbian and Gay Chorus

CHORUS

See listing in "Classical Music."

Movie Soundtracks

rec.music.movies

Soundtracks are key to the music lover these days, with *E.T.*'s John Williams and *Batman*'s Danny Elfman—who both get plenty of space here—the kings of the heap. Loads of trivia, "Good Score/Bad Movie" discussion, trivia, rare recordings, and trivia. Need help finding a soundtrack or figuring out who you heard in the background of your favorite blockbuster? rec.music.movies is the stop for you. For more info on Elfman, see "Oingo Boingo" in "Rock and Pop."

soundtracks

Discussions, reviews, and availability of specific soundtracks in all formats, as well as publication of trading lists and hardware for film music reproduction.

Contact soundtracks-request@ifi.unizh.ch (Michel Hafner)

Musical Instrument Conservation and Technology

MICAT-L

A unique forum that addresses "matters of joint interest to the fields of objects conservation and musical instrument technology." Discussions may include technology and manufacturing of musical instruments, techniques of conservation, restoration, and scientific examination. MICAT-L is a perfect example of the Net's ability to focus on particular combinations of musical and technological culture.

Code M

Owner or Contact Cary Karp, micat-l-request@nrm.se

To Subscribe E-mail mailserv@nrm.se; in the body of the message, type **SUBSCRIBE MICAT-L** followed by your real name. To unsubscribe, send the command **UNSUBSCRIBE MICAT-L** in e-mail to mailserv@nrm.se. Send all other list-related commands to mailserv@nrm.se. For assistance, send the command **HELP**. Send all articles to MICAT-L@nrm.se.

I recommend the following Website as a starting place for this section, for the simple reason that it's so wonderfully diverse.

Musical Resources on the Internet

http://www.music.indiana.edu/misc/music_resources.html

The Indiana School of Music houses one of the most complete databases for Internet music resources. You could actually begin at http://www.music. indiana.edu/, where you can link to IU's music library and various music departments, as well as track down general info about the campus. Click in to their Music Resources, however, for academic sites—from Accordion to Zamir Chorale of Boston—Gopher and FTP servers, user-maintained information, as well as nonacademic and geographical sites. Their artist-specific listing tends toward the pop acts, but holds a remarkable cross-section of artists nonetheless.

From snooping around this site, I discovered just weeks before the ceremony that the Grammys went online for the first time in 1995, with a soon-to-be-announced URL for updates and information. Keep checking for more info.

Musical Theater

MUSICALS

The place for shared experience, ideas, thoughts, and comments about Broadway, community theater, and college musicals. From *Guys and Dolls* to *The Will Rogers Follies*, cast albums to television, good actresses to bad actors, MUSICALS encourages any and all discussion; most interest seems to lie in gossip, upcoming performance dates, and ticket prices.

Owner or Contact Elizabeth Lear Newman, eliz@world.std.com

To Subscribe E-mail Majordomo@world.std.com; in the body of the message, type **SUBSCRIBE MUSICALS**. To unsubscribe, e-mail Majordomo@world.std.com; in the body of the message, type **UNSUBSCRIBE MUSICALS**. Send all other list-related commands to Majordomo@world.std.com. For assistance, send the command **HELP**. Send all articles to MUSICALS@world.std.com.

A Musical Resources' Sampler

My only frustration with music_resources' is that its listings appear in no particular order: Jazz, ethnic, drums and percussion page, schools, Croatian music, Renaissance instruments—it's all here if you look. Plenty of unexpected stops, too: "The Death of Rock and Roll: Untimely Demises, Morbid Preoccupations, And Premature Forecasts Of Doom," profiled earlier in the section, is cross-referenced at this site.

Just a fraction of the listings you'll find at http://www.music.indiana.edu/:

American Recordings	Grand Royal Records
Ballet of Austin	JUKENET, The Internet Music Store
Caroline Records	Music Industry Contact List
C/Z Records	Rocky Mountain Ragtime Festival
Canadian Music Exchange	San Jose Symphony
Colorado Mahler Festival	Songs of the Abayudaya Jews of Uganda
Electronic Music Software Via FTP	Techno/Rave Archives
Geffen Records	*VIBE* Magazine

rec.arts.theatre.musicals

Was *Phantom of the Opera* lip-synched? Who's subbing the lead role in *Miss Saigon*? These and other pertinent on- and off-Broadway theatrical questions find answers on rec.arts.theatre.musicals. From *Thoroughly Modern Millie* to *Les Miserables* and *Grease*, this is your front-row ticket for musical theater on the Internet.

Musical Theatre Collaborations

COLLAB-L

A unique list that brings playwrights, directors, theater technicians, composers and librettists together for the purpose of collaborative new scripts for performance. Ongoing and quickly changing discussions.

Owner or Contact Steve Schrum, SAS14@psu.edu

To Subscribe Send a politely worded request to the list owner or contact shown above.

Michael Nesmith

http://www.primenet.com/~flex/nesmith.html

Pulse! magazine recently referred to Nesmith—the one-time Monkee who's been recording music and challenging pop culture since 1965—as a "country-pop-eccentric-cum-media-visionary." I'm not sure if they meant it as a compliment, but this Website nonetheless houses an awesome array of his work, including discographies and biographies, up-to-date Nez Newz, and his current touring status. Besides links to Monkees and Hellecasters home pages, you can also access info on pre-Monkees recordings, view covers of Nesmith's sheet music, and read concert set lists and interviews, from TV to the *Dallas Morning News*. The term "cult following" springs to mind....

Rock and Roll Digital Gallery

http://www.hooked.net/julianne/index.html

This eye-popping site features rock and roll poster art, some of the best I've found yet. In addition to great old works for artists such as The Doors and 13th

Floor Elevators (see Figure 2.33), you can get information about the Avalon Ballroom Series Screensaver for Windows, which features 33 posters created by such greats as Stanley Mouse and Alton Kelley.

If you're into rock postering from a more current era, check out Frank Kozik's exhibition on "Addicted To Noise," described later in "Calendars and Magazines."

You'll find many more great music tidbits on the hooked server: BuzzNet (described later in "Calendars and Magazines") maintains a fine online magazine with music-related topics, and other artists from the San Francisco Bay area are beginning to spring up. Keep the hooked URL handy.

Figure 2.33:
Musical pleasures for your eyes: Art from the Rock and Roll Digital Gallery

Space Music

SPACE-MUSIC

Lots of new artists use electronic instrumentation to create floating soundscapes—musical compositions that grow organically, transporting the listener to a cosmic, ambient place. The most frequently discussed artists on this list include Klaus Schulze, Steve Roach, Robert Rich, and Micheal Stearns. Let yourself go....

Code D

Owner or Contact Dave Datta (datta@cs.uwp.edu)

To Subscribe Send a polite message to space-music-request@cs.uwp.edu asking to be added to the mailing list. Please include your real name. Send all other commands to space-music-request@cs.uwp.edu. Send articles to space-music@cs.uwp.edu.

Vocal Singing

VOCALIST

Students and experienced teachers as well as ordinary laypeople and those who want to know more about techniques, practicing, voice care, repertoire, auditions, concerts, and records, tune in to VOCALIST, which enjoys listings from all over the world.

Code D

Owner or Contact Marko Hotti, mhotti@paju.oulu.fi

To Subscribe E-mail Majordomo@phoenix.oulu.fi; in the body of the message, type **SUBSCRIBE VOCALIST**. To unsubscribe, send the command **UNSUBSCRIBE VOCALIST** in e-mail to Majordomo@phoenix.oulu.fi. Send all other list-related commands to Majordomo@phoenix.oulu.fi. For assistance, send the command **HELP**. Send all articles to VOCALIST@phoenix.oulu.fi.

Tom Waits

http://www.nwu.edu/waits

Truly a Renaissance man of our generation, reclusive and gravelly-voiced Tom Waits has distinguished himself as a fine musician and actor whose work is constantly evolving. His Website is simple and complete: It features an exhaustive discography—with nearly twenty solo works and countless collaborative recordings—filmography—*Dracula, Cotton Club, Down By Law, Ironweed,* and *Short Cuts,* to name but a few—and bibliography of works about him. You can also investigate his musical influences, view his album covers and a few other assorted GIFs, and read about his rare concert appearances. A favorite artist of mine; a great stop.

Musicians' Resources

The Internet is based on a *DIY*—Do It Yourself—ethic, and working musicians will find it an excellent resource for specific information about their chosen instrument. Although many entries in this section reflect sources for computer-based music—programmable keyboards and instruments that use similar programs—the electric and acoustic musician will find valuable information as well.

This section exemplifies the Internet's ability to serve the individual PC user: While several thousand Net surfers may jack in to a particular Website as fans of an artist, perhaps a few hundred will track down the mailing list devoted to those who play the didgeridoo. Yet both are accessible with equal ease.

Rather than recommend starting places in this section, I've tried instead to compile a broad range of entry-level listings for a variety of instruments. Any of the following entries should be perfectly suited as jumping-off points.

Acoustic Guitar Archive

ftp.casbah.acns.nwu.edu

Look inside .pub, then under acoustic-guitar for *Acoustic Guitar Digest*, with tabulature, history, and other tidbits for the non-electric guitar enthusiast. Frequent Eric Clapton references.

Acoustic Guitarists

rec.music.makers.guitar.acoustic

Less gear here than at the FTP site, and more technique: Finger-picking, faster playing, hand squeaking, and Carpal Tunnel/RSI information. Frequent Steve James references.

Bagpipe Players

BAGPIPE

See description in "International and Ethnic Music."

Bass Players

rec.music.makers.bass

I wouldn't know an Ibanez Tube Screamer if I heard—saw? ran over?—one, but bass guitar players evidently will. Plenty of for-sales, advice on acoustical and electrical questions, and technical explanations for intricate basslines within Red Hot Chili Peppers, Mike Watt, and fIREHOSE songs. Check out the "Raw Fingers Advice" posting.

Bassoon and Oboe

DOUBLEREED-L

This double-reed list provides a forum for performers, teachers, and students. Its topics include music, reed-making, performances, instruments, care, clinics, workshops, and festivals for music of the oboe, English horn, bassoon, and contrabassoon.

Code U (For a description of these codes, see "Mailing List Codes" in "Classical Music.")

Owner or Contact Rodney Boyd, zzboyr@acc.wuacc.edu

To Subscribe E-mail LISTSERV@acc.wuacc.edu; in the body of the message, type **SUBSCRIBE DOUBLEREED-L** followed by your real name. To unsubscribe, send the command **UNSUB DOUBLEREED-L** in e-mail to LISTSERV@acc.wuacc.edu. Send all other list-related commands to LISTSERV@acc.wuacc.edu. Send all articles to DOUBLEREED-L@acc.wuacc.edu.

Brass Musical Instruments

BRASS

Trumpeters, trombonists, and other brass players interested in performance and related topics, "especially small musical ensembles," can find info here. A good source for sheet music and upcoming competitions.

Code D

Owner or Contact Ted Zateslo, brass-request@geomag.gly.fsu.edu

To Subscribe or unsubscribe, send a politely worded request to brass-request@geomag.gly.fsu.edu; be sure to include your real name in the request, which will be handled by a human being. Information on submitting articles to the mailing list will be provided upon subscription.

Often within a mailing list, newsgroup, or Website, you'll find subcategories of subjects that can tighten your focus. If you don't see your particular instrument listed here, try searching a more general subject.

Chapman Stick

STICKY-FINGER

See description in "Beyond Category."

Classical Guitar

rec.music.classical.guitar

See description in "Classical Music."

Cyberdog Music Database

http://www.magicnet.net/rz/three_minute_dog/cyberdog.html

This site is an excellent resource for the up-and-coming alternative musician seeking information about touring, support, publicity, and promotion. For a more complete description, see the listing in "Alternative Music."

DJs Services

BPM-Request

This is a general list, entitled *Beats Per Minute*, designed for club DJs and other mixologists.

To Subscribe E-mail bpm-request@andrew.cmu.edu.

DJ List

This list covers relevant topics for college-radio DJs, including station policies and equipment training.

To Subscribe E-mail LISTSERV@VM1.NODAK.EDU; in the body of the message, type **SUB DJ-L** with your full name.

Electronic Music

EMUSIC-L
EMUSIC-D

Two lists in one—EMUSIC-L for undigested mail, and EMUSIC-D for a moderately edited digest—devoted to electronic music, including "synthesis methods, algo-

---

"Mine Goes Up To 11"

If ever a movie was made that had the working rock and roll musician in mind, it's the decade-old *This Is Spinal Tap*, the pseudo-documentary of a British heavy metal band. Responsible for the ensuing smash soundtrack, sold-out tour, and, most recently, a double CD-ROM with outtakes and commentary from "band members" and director Rob Reiner, no rock parody has ever matched *Spinal Tap*'s success.

Spinal Tap lives on on the Internet, with their own newsgroup (see "Rock and Pop") where you can discuss at length either the movie or the band itself, from particular body parts related to the film to the infamous cucumber scene, which must be seen to be appreciated.

Spinal Tap's forthcoming Web page promises samples, interviews, and, of course, a volume knob that goes up to 11. Whether you're a working musician or simply have a keen appreciation for parody of an already outrageous medium like rock and roll, check out the movie (or the CD-ROM) and click into alt.fan.spinal-tap.

rithmic composition, psychoacoustics, timbral research, instrument design, MIDI troubleshooting, new tricks for old machines, reviews of current and historical musical and technical trends, homegrown sounds and software."

Code D, U

Owner or Contact Eric Harnden, eharnden@auvm.american.edu.

To Subscribe E-mail LISTSERV@auvm.american.edu; in the body of the message, type **SUBSCRIBE EMUSIC-L** followed by your real name. To unsubscribe, send the command **UNSUBSCRIBE EMUSIC-L** in e-mail to LISTSERV@auvm.american.edu. Send all other list-related commands to LISTSERV@auvm.american.edu. For assistance, send the command **HELP**. Send all articles to EMUSIC-L@auvm.american.edu. To obtain a list of file archives, send the command INDEX E-MAIL-D to LISTSERV@auvm.american.edu.

Electronic Musicians

alt.emusic

See description in "Alternative Music."

Guitar Players

rec.music.makers.guitar

With more focus on electric than rec.music.makers.guitar.acoustic, the guitar group offers tube supplier addresses, custom-built amplifier instructions, and copyright help, plus the latest on Stratocaster reissues, Les Paul copies, and pedal steels. Even more frequent Eric Clapton references.

Don't forget: Not all Internet service providers are connected to all newsgroups. If you want to access one that your network isn't linked to, contact your system administrator and ask if it can be added.

Handbell

HANDBELL-L

The handbell list is open to all enthusiasts, including ringers and directors, and whether you're a *tune ringer* or a *change ringer*—and only a handbell player can tell you for sure—you're welcome here.

Code D, U

Owner or Contact Jason B. Tiller, jtiller@ringer.jpl.nasa.gov

To Subscribe E-mail HANDBELL-L@ringer.jpl.nasa.gov; in the subject of the message, type **SUBSCRIBE**. To unsubscribe, send the command **UNSUBSCRIBE** in the subject of an e-mail to HANDBELL-L@ringer.jpl.nasa.gov. Send all articles to HANDBELL-L@ringer.jpl.nasa.gov.

Harpsichords and Related Topics

HPSCHD-L

With focus on all early stringed keyboard instruments, including harpsichords, clavichords, fortepianos, virginals, and all similar instruments except the modern piano, this list is open to myriad topics, from history to construction, performing, practice, literature, pedagogy, care, and ownership.

Owner or Contact Dave Kelzenberg, dkelzenb@blue.weeg.uiowa.edu, Ben Chi, bec@albany.edu

To Subscribe E-mail LISTSERV@albany.edu; in the body of the message, type **SUBSCRIBE HPSCHD-L** followed by your real name. To unsubscribe, send the command **UNSUBSCRIBE HPSCHD-L** in e-mail to LISTSERV@albany.edu. Send all other list-related commands to LISTSERV@albany.edu. For assistance, send the command **HELP**. Send all articles to HPSCHD-L@albany.edu.

Lute Music

LUTE

Enjoying the resurgence of interest in Baroque and other pre-classical musical styles, lutenists can find an excellent source of information about their instrument on the Internet.

Code D

Owner or Contact Wayne Cripps, wbc@cs.dartmouth.edu

To Subscribe Send a politely worded request to lute-request@cs.dartmouth.edu. To unsubscribe, send a politely worded request to lute-request@cs.dartmouth.edu. Information on where to send articles will be provided upon subscribing.

Marching Band/Drum and Bugle Corps

alt.colorguard
rec.arts.marching.colorguard
rec.arts.marching.drumcorps
rec.arts.marching.misc

A good way to keep track of equipment suppliers, competition dates, and members of Drum Corps International.

MIDI File Trading and Collaboration

NetJam

A cool idea: NetJam offers a venue for online musical collaboration through trading MIDI files. A subscriber who receives a file can muck around with it, resend it, and await reactions. As you might expect, NetJam requires more than a little technical knowledge, but struck me as utterly hospitable to the newbie. If you want, ask for a FAQ before you get in too deep.

Contact netjam-request@xcf.berkeley.edu Craig Latta

Music Journalists

alt.music.journalism

A resource for the music writer, alt.music.journalism is a well balanced mix of job offerings (ranging in genre from Classical to Industrial, from writers for established industry journals to cartoonists for fledgling online 'zines), services, and casual discussion for those in the field.

If you want to know when your favorite artist will release his or her next CD, check the future release listing, which runs a few months in advance and appears to be regularly updated. Covering artists from Henry Rollins to Bruce Springsteen, this listing may prove to be one of your most comprehensive sources for upcoming recordings. You'll also find companies hawking and designing interactive press kits, news about alternative music publications, information about alternative radio stations, and directions to the Tap Room, a "virtual pub for finding out what's new around the country in 'lifestyle' topics, including music and nightclubbing."

Evidently, alt.music.journalism *is one of those newsgroups that may be difficult to access from some providers. It's worth tracking down, though, if you write about music.*

Music Library

IAML-L

With listings in English, French, or German, IAML-L is an online music library maintained by members of The International Association of Music Libraries, Archives and Documentation Centers. Nonmembers, including music publishers and dealers interested in the wealth of catalogued information, are welcome to subscribe. Communications may be addressed to it by "anyone (except commercial advertisers) who so desires."

Code U

Owner or Contact Postmaster@nrm.se

To Subscribe Send a politely worded request to IAML-Request@nrm.se. To unsubscribe, send a politely worded request to IAML-Request@nrm.se. Send all articles to IAML-L@nrm.se.

Music Makers

rec.music.makers

With more pop focus than the rec.music.compose newsgroup discussed later in this section, rec.music.makers worries less about theory and more about the music biz: Lots of listings for equipment, musicians, and road managers wanted;

small- and large-scale touring info; copyright laws; and record pressing tips. Also listings seeking industry lawyers, guitar effects suggestions, and times and places for jam sessions.

Music Producers

alt.music.producer

A crash-course in sampling laws and job market reports, this newsgroup for music producers feels a bit like an industry boardroom meeting in Downtown L.A., but its professional bent is a welcome change from the ramblings and cursings on a typical fan group. All this talk about "market share" and "units sold" is pretty far from my musical leanings, but as a source for recent release schedules and—they promise—future online reports from *Billboard* magazine, alt.music.producer is valuable and well maintained.

Musical Equipment

rec.music.makers.marketplace

See description in "Special Collectors' Section."

Musical Instrument Conservation and Technology

MICAT-L

See description in "Beyond Category."

Musical Instrument Designers and Builders

rec.music.makers.builders

"Dedicated to the discussion of designing, building, and repairing any device intended to make music," says the FAQ: "Percussive, string, wind, keyboard, experimental, acoustic, electric, electronic, amplificatory, robotic, and ridiculous." Listings include addresses of parts suppliers for soundboards, hammered dulcimer tuners, trussrods, didgeridoo, and timpani; an address for the essential *Experimental Musical Instruments* newsletter; blurbs on the master instru-ventor Harry Partch; and a forum on "routing the guitar binding channel." Remember: DIY means *Do It Yourself.*

For more information about a major artist who has been experimenting with his own homemade instruments for years, investigate http://www.nwu.edu/waits.

Musical Software

Smallmusic

Here's the list's description: "...formed to discuss and develop an object-oriented software system for music. The current environment is Smalltalk 80." Got that? Got a clue? Go for it.

Contact smallmusic-request@xcf.berkeley.edu (Craig Latta)

Musicians and Composers

rec.music.compose

The group whose focus is for "writers of musical and classical works" makes room for composers from pop to classical. A broad mix of theory (via software, books, or discussion), job openings, and music festival listings balance some interesting philosophical discussions: One popular thread is "Psychology Of Pop Music." Maybe Sting could contribute to that one.

Percussionists

rec.music.makers.percussion

This newsgroup for drummers and percussionists, like the other music.makers', focuses primarily on techniques and equipment, from "Conga Care and Feeding" to Billy Cobham and Charlie Watts. Enough brand name arguments to keep things lively.

Pianists

rec.music.makers.piano

Besides the expected, you'll find info on moving and storing your piano, finding a teacher, reaching a tuner or repairman, buying sheet music, and suggested exercises. Also player-piano rolls for sale or trade, and arguments over the qualities of digital instruments.

Pipe Organs

PIPORG-L

This list features musical, technical, and historical information on organs of all kinds: Classical, theater, electronic, reed, tracker, and electropneumatic. Topics including past and future recitals, recordings, jobs wanted and available, restoration hints, and projects are all encouraged.

"Electropneumatic?" Sounds like a medical rehabilitation technique to me.

Owner or Contact Dave Schutt, schutt@netcom.com, Ben Chi, BEC@ALBNYVM1. BITNET

To Subscribe E-mail LISTSERV@albany.edu; in the body of the message, type **SUBSCRIBE PIPORG-L** followed by your real name. To unsubscribe, send the command **UNSUB PIPORG-L** in e-mail to LISTSERV@albany.edu. Send all other list-related commands to LISTSERV@albany.edu. Send all articles to PIPORG-L@ albany.edu.

Synthesizers

rec.music.makers.synth

I couldn't see much difference between rec.music.makers.synth and alt.emusic; but the synth site seems to favor MIDI samplers, latest software versions, FTP sites, and plenty of merchandise for sale or trade.

Scottish Drumming

SIDEDRUM

See description in "International and Ethnic Music."

If you don't see your instrument of choice on this list, I'd suggest a Gopher or FTP search by the instrument's name. You're likely to turn up a variety of related sources, including some lists, newsgroups, and Websites.

Special Collectors' Section

Cool stuff! Here's where you'll find the best in CDs, rare vinyl, rock and roll merchandise, and collectables. Most entries offer merchandise for sale, but some (usually private) listings offer items for barter or trade. You can also request free online and snail-mail catalogues brimming with things to buy.

The relative smallness of this section reflects two things about the Internet: First, its tendency toward informational sources rather than commercial ones; second, the fact that the Internet hasn't—to a large degree—been discovered yet as a place to sell things. The coming commerciality is inevitable. However, whether it's a good or bad thing remains to be seen.

Like those in Musicians' Resources, any listing in this section is a good starting place designed to cater to the newbie. Happy hunting!

Audio Binaries Database

alt.binaries.sounds.music

Not a newsgroup in the strictest sense, alt.binaries.sounds.music is where you'll find distribution of encoded music files for everything ranging from Billy Joel's "Piano Man" to movie soundtracks to minuets from "L'Arlesienne." Whatever playback method you can boot—.MOD, .WAV, .AU—there's something for you. Don't have a clue what I'm talking about? Check the FAQ file and peruse the listings for playback software available for your download.

Their list of contributors seems to be growing rapidly—as the range from children's songs to pop hits indicates—and is worth the trouble to scan through. There's something comfortingly human about hearing your computer play back George Clinton's "Atomic Dog" after a 13-part download.

Since the artists receive no compensation from your copy of their songs, the question, of course, is whether alt.binaries.sounds.music*'s available files violate copyright law. Get 'em while you can.*

.AU, .AIFF, .AIFC, .AAAGH!

As you remember from Part One, audio files' names include *extensions* that correspond to their required playback software (See Part One, Fig. 1.3). The following list will help you recognize those various audio file extensions. Be sure to choose formats your machine can support.

.AIF, .AIFF, .AIFC	Apple or SGI audio file
.AU	NeXT or Sun audio file
.IFF, .MOD, .NST	Amiga audio file
.SND	PC, Macintosh, NeXT, or Sun audio file
.VOC	SoundBlaster audio file
.WAV	MS Windows audio file

Found a provocative audio file that's in a format you can't support? Numerous *conversion* applications alter the file's format so you can play it back on your PC. The most popular conversion files are:

SOX	SOund eXchange, found at ftp.cwi.nl/pub/audio/SOX5dos.zip
WHAM	Waveform Hold And Modify, found at ftp.ncsa.uiuc.edu/Web/Mosaic/Windows/Viewers/Wham131.zip
Wplany	an audio player for PC speaker, found at ftp.ncsa.uiuc.edu/PC/Mosaic/Viewers/wplny09b.zip

More and more often, you'll find sound files formatted **.MPG** or **.MPE**, which are variations on **.MPEG**: MPEG stands for *Motion Picture Experts Group*, and MPEG files were once strictly used for animation. But audiophiles—forgive me, I couldn't resist—found the accompanying sound quality to be excellent, and MPEG may someday prove to be the industry standard. The extremely popular IUMA site (See "Alternative Music") uses MPEG audio. You can find an MPEG player on IUMA or at ftp.ncsa.uiuc.edu/Web/Mosaic/Windows/viewers/mpeg32h.zip.

Those types of audio files (also called *sound* files) discussed in alt.binaries.sounds.music are the same as others you'll find throughout the Internet.

CD Collectors

rec.music.cd

It's a music fair online! Catalogues, rarities, free music database programs—it's your best source for digitally recorded discs, as well as quirky discussions, including how to repair CD scratches, how to find lists of discographies and new releases, and how much everybody hates those two-in-one CD cases.

Don't squander your nest egg investing in a Metallica boxed set so rare it doesn't actually exist. As on any Internet stop, make sure that the companies listed in rec.music.cd *are legitimate before sending your credit card numbers: Precede your order with some research (or e-mail a few fellow Netizens) to investigate the company you're buying from. But you already knew that....*

CD*now!* Online Music Store

http://www.cdnow.com/

With over 100,000 titles and 140,000 CDs, cassettes, videos, and T-shirts, CD*now!* (see Figure 2.34) is the quintessential Internet music retail resource. Known for their huge classical store, CD*now!* incorporates a browser that can search for titles by name, often uncovering half a dozen matching titles in the process. Their Pop and Country sections include artists' current biographies, track listings, and a 1-to-4 star rating system; To "put it in your shopping basket," simply click on the item you want. CD*now!* requires no minimum purchase, takes a variety of payment methods, is open twenty-four hours, and claims to deliver their goods in three to six business days.

In addition, the site's "All-Music Guide Forum" (see Figure 2.35) provides two huge databases: One for "the largest collection of substantive album reviews ever assembled" and another of music magazines' profiles. My only complaints about the online supermarket were its slow loading time and occasional tendency to disconnect me, but overall I was impressed.

Figure 2.34:
CDnow! is the Internet's quintessential retail source for recordings, a Website with over 100,000 titles in all formats.

Figure 2.35:
CDnow!'s All-Music Guide Forum provides reviews of recordings and magazines.

CDs and CD Players

InfoCD

A generic mailing list for information about compact discs and their players; a good hub for sales information, upcoming innovations, and addresses and URLs for other CD-related connections.

To Subscribe E-mail cdrequest@cisco.nosc.mil.

DAT-Heads

http://www.atd.ucar.edu/rdp/dat-heads

There are general Websites and specific ones: DAT-Heads (see Figure 2.36) offers advice and provides ongoing discussion about how Digital Audio Tape and DAT playback decks can be used for bootlegging live recordings of Grateful Dead and Phish concerts. Ooooookay?

Figure 2.36:
An Internet site with a particular mission: DAT-Heads fills you in on how to best bootleg a Dead concert.

General Music Collectables

rec.music.marketplace

The marketplace here is for those seeking records, tapes, and CDs, as well as other gear and back-issues of music magazines, particularly those that feature CD reviews. No musical equipment, but plenty of oldies, reissues, the newest of the new, used—everything here, in all formats, unlike what you'll find at rec.music.cd. The only problem with having a music store in your living room is that you can't preview what you buy first; maybe that will change with time. In the meantime, don't forget to do your detective work before plunking down the cash....

Music Video Collectors

rec.music.video

At rec.music.video you'll find everything from live Aerosmith tapes to exercise videos, as well as updated FTP sites and plenty of opinionated pro- and con-MTV viewers. Many more "Videos Wanted" than those available—this seems like a specialized stop where readers jump off once they've found their rare Pearl Jam VHS.

Musical Equipment

rec.music.makers.marketplace

A venue for buying and selling music-making equipment, whether acoustic or electric: Microphones, cases, keyboards, racks, instruments of all kinds. More Equipment Wanteds/Offers to Sell than you can imagine. Get out that wallet....

78 RPM Record Collectors

78-L

Remember those thick slabs of plastic in your grandfather's record library? This discussion list dedicated to the pre-LP has info for rarities, catalogues, and collectables of all kinds, including gramophones and other 78 RPM players.

Sound Card Resources

comp.sys.ibm.pc.soundcard.music

That long address translates to "Music on IBM(-like) PC soundcards." Since a PC must have an installed sound card in order for you to listen to music files on the Internet (see the "Hardware" and "Software" sections of Part One), you may find this a necessary group to join. Here you'll find reprints of *Keyboard* articles, FTP sites for .MOD and other files, and many cross-references to track down just what you need or questions you have. You may be a little confused, initially, puttering around comp.sys.ibm.pc.soundcard.music, but I think you'll find this newsgroup to be an excellent companion to this book.

I was also given the URL http://www.creaf.com/www/sbvalue_specs.html *as a source for digital audio information, including specifications of players and download-able copies of playback software. Although I could never access the site, people assure me it's possible. I pass it on to you as another possible audio file source.*

Calendars and Magazines

As the Internet becomes more and more accessible, many users are turning to it to introduce electronic magazines, books, and guides—publications previously reserved strictly for the print medium. Your final stop on the Pocket Tour gathers the best of these new media, reflecting an area of the Net guaranteed to boom in the next few years.

From rock magazines to community music calendars, online publications are springing up faster than I can document, much in the way local cable TV access took off several years ago. If you don't see listings in this section for your particular musical interests, investigate other more-familiar sources: The venues or organizations that promote the music you like, the radio stations that play it, the stores that sell it. Ask them if they're wired to the Internet. Often you'll discover a fledgling publication right under your nose.

ONLINE CALENDARS

Austin, Texas Music Calendar

austin.music

The most in-depth regional guide I found, this Austin newsgroup offers a detailed walk through the up-and-coming Texas musical epicenter. Who's recording at Antone's? Who's playing at the Continental Club? Broken Spoke? La Zona Rosa? Emo's? You'll also find plenty of equipment, musician, and live schedule listings.

Bay Area/San Francisco Music Calendar

ba.music

The San Francisco Bay Area music listings are widely focused: Ad listings for equipment and musicians-needed, as well as calendars for upcoming events from Reverend Horton Heat at a local punk club to the Marin Light Opera schedule.

The List Music Calendar

the-list-request

Run by "punks with presses," this Berkeley-based nonprofit publication gathers a huge list of every funk/punk/thrash/ska show in Northern California (and a few listings in Nevada and Oregon), updates it every Friday, and mails it out. The electronic version arrives in Unix format. Subscribers get a huge slab of data, but it's up-to-date, with notes for recommended shows, cancellations, and the essential "pit warning."

To Subcribe E-mail the-list-request@violet.berkeley.edu.

Regional Music Newsgroups

More and more potential audience members are jacking in to local Internet servers as sources for musical event listings. The following are specific local newsgroups available as this book goes to press. A Gopher search should turn up even more listings—perhaps some for your region.

- cle.music (Cleveland, OH)
- dc.music (Washington, DC)
- houston.music (Houston, TX)
- Nashville.general (Nashville, TN)
- pdx.music (Portland.OR)
- phl.music (Philadelphia, PA)
- sdnet.music (San Diego, CA)
- tamu.music (Texas A&M University)
- um.music (University of Maryland)

I recommend the following newsgroup, rec.music.reviews, *as a starting place for budding music journalists. What better medium in which to have your first published work appear than the Internet?*

South By Southwest Music Conference

http://monsterbit.com/sxsw.html

Look for conferences' and festivals' use of online resources to increase dramatically: This year's South By Southwest Music and Media Conference held in Austin, TX, offered initial info via their e-mail address (72662.2465@compuserve.com), and just started their online site.

Woodstock '94

FESTIVAL

Mudstock—er, Woodstock '94 fostered a brand-new generation of flower children who, besides preferring Nine Inch Nails to Jimi Hendrix, are also way wired. The public library in Saugerties, NY, has created FESTIVAL for discussing last year's event, and continues to maintain the site to answer after-the-fact questions about the community and its public-interest activities.

Code M

Owner or Contact Jane Letus, Woodstk1@nysernet.org

To Subscribe E-mail LISTSERV@nysernet.org; in the body of the message, type **SUBSCRIBE FESTIVAL** followed by your real name. To unsubscribe, send the command **UNSUB FESTIVAL** in e-mail to LISTSERV@nysernet.org. Send all other list-related commands to LISTSERV@nysernet.org. Send all articles to FESTIVAL@nysernet.org.

ONLINE MAGAZINES

Addicted To Noise Online Rock Magazine

http://www.addict.com/ATN/

Colliding *Rolling Stone*, *Spin*, and *Spy*, *Addicted To Noise* wraps rock journalism in remarkable graphics and delivers it online. Hotlinked to the popular IUMA site (see description in "Alternative Music"), the six-month-old electronic magazine combines traditional layout with the best in digitally rendered eye and ear candy.

With graphics, video clips, and audio files available for downloading, *ATN* (see Figure 2.37) begins with an editorial and e-mail "Letters" section, a newbie FAQ file, and a navigational "Help Guide." Readers can browse digital art galleries or read CD reviews while listening to sound snippets from the recordings themselves. Music-industry advertising money makes *ATN*'s "Sponsors" section (see Figure 2.38) as appealing as its feature pages, offering a full platter of artists' GIFs, QuickTime videos, soundbytes, and available music files, all playable using IUMA software.

Cool. Look for a dozen clones in the future. (See "New Magazines, a New Medium.")

Figure 2.37:
Welcome to Addicted To Noise, the best of the new online rock magazines.

BuzzNet Online Magazine

http://www.insomnia.com/buzznet/gindex.html

With a focus on alternative culture, San Francisco-based *BuzzNet* scrutinizes a wide cross-section of influential books and 'zines, counter-culture personalities and music.

Start by clicking on the home page's "Beats" icon (see Figure 2.39), beneath which you'll find a variety of features and foci, from a locally produced Noise Pop Festival of punk bands to a long article on the New British Invasion (and the likes of Massive Attack, Wolfgang Press, and Portishead) as well as a great interview with legendary producer Bill Laswell. Two columns, the "State of the 7-Inch" and "Letter From New York," address seven-inch singles and the hip-hop scene respectively; you also can link to *FAD* magazine and local commercial-alternative radio station KITS-FM. A hopping hive.

Figure 2.38:
ATN's "Sponsors" section includes plenty of downloadable GIFs
and QuickTime video clips.

I tried repeatedly to reach Insomnia Records, an alternative music mail-order mecca whose remarkable print catalogue lists its URL at the www.insomnia.com *server, but could never locate it.*

Consumable Online Electronic Magazine

CONSUMABLE

A good-sized electronic magazine in mailing list form that offers a good balance of reviews, interviews, and "offbeat commentary." Sent out every two weeks, *Consumable* is centered on alternative rock, but willing to consider other formats.

Figure 2.39:
The BuzzNet Welcome screen: Click on "Beats"
to delve into its musical offerings.

New Magazines, a New Medium

Originally envisioning *Addicted To Noise* in CD-ROM format until a glimpse of budding Mosaic software and a visit to the IUMA site convinced him of the Web's capabilities, editor and publisher Michael Goldberg sees his online magazine as the next step in music publications.

"I think *ATN* combines the best of journalism with the capabilities of multimedia," he says from his virtual West Coast office: "This medium allows you to do so much more than a print magazine."

Each issue's "cover package" features a subject—from R.E.M.'s world tour to rock poster artist Frank Kozik—treated to numerous articles, interviews, and reviews. This in-depth coverage is the first of several advantages Goldberg sees in an electronic medium.

"Because there's no space limitation, we can include a five-section special report on

Owner or Contact Bob Gajarsky, gajarsky@pilot.njin.net

To Subscribe Send a politely worded request to gajarsky@pilot.njin.net. To unsubscribe, send a politely worded request to gajarsky@pilot.njin.net.

ePulse Online Magazine

EPULSE-L

Tower Records' fledgling e-magazine is still learning to crawl, but you'll find interesting Top-10 lists, Net happenings (and directions to find them), features on audio/video gear, contests, and loads of free stuff. Look for *ePulse* to provide more in-depth coverage of many subjects covered in *PULSE!*, the long-time print version.

To Subscribe E-mail **subscribe epulse-l** to listserv@netcom.com. To unsubscribe, forward the message **unsubscribe epulse-l** to listserv@netcom.com.

iMpulse Music Journal

IMPULSE

A broadly focused journal of music news, reviews, information, and opinion delivered monthly to list subscribers. While its coverage centers on commercial the MC5," he explains. "If people don't want to read 20,000 words on the Beach Boys or on the MC5, they don't have to, but it's there for rock fans who want an online resource."

Likewise, *ATN*'s constantly updated "Music News of the World" reflects the immediacy of the Net: "As soon as we post an item on 'Music News'," Goldberg says, "we instantly reach people all over the world. When Eddie Vedder's [recent] live radio broadcast in Seattle ended at 11PM," he recalls, "we had our news story online between 12 and 1AM."

His masthead already bursting with many reputable writers and photographers, Goldberg—an editor at *Rolling Stone*—knows that editorial rants, searing graphics, and a smorgasbord of available files alone won't make the fledgling e-zine a success. "Whether it's an online publication, a TV show, or a book, content is key to anything," he says. "Packaging is secondary. Our idea is to use this medium as creatively as possible to present the best in rock journalism."

alternative music, it also seems to have plenty of room for other musical subjects, both pop and esoteric.

Owner or Contact Richard F. Crum, rfcrum@clark.net, Roger L. Yee, ryee@dsi group.com

To Subscribe E-mail IMPULSE@dsigroup.com; in the subject of the message, type **SUBSCRIBE IMPULSE**. To unsubscribe, e-mail IMPULSE@dsigroup.com; in the subject of the message, type **UNSUBSCRIBE IMPULSE**. Send all submissions to IMPULSE@dsigroup.com. To receive the iMpulse Music Journal FAQ, e-mail IMPULSE @dsigroup.com and in the subject line write in all caps GET IMPULSE INFO. If you are interested in submitting articles for publication, e-mail IMPULSE@dsi group.com and in the subject line write in all caps GET WRITER INFO.

OTHER PUBLICATIONS

CD and Record Reviews

rec.music.reviews

Always wanted to be a published record reviewer without waiting for editors to return your calls? Just drop them off here, where you're almost guaranteed a readership. Reviews of performances, genres, records, and CDs, artists' profiles, and pointers to local scenes fill out the listings. The writing is good, for the most part. It's a small newsgroup now, but undoubtedly growing—a good place to hone your skills under the scrutinous eyes of the Net reader.

CUNY Music Programs

CUNYMUS

In lieu of congregating on a campus, students from the Graduate Center of the City University of New York (CUNY) exchange ideas on the internet. CUNYMUS' purpose is "to provide students in a doctoral program with discussions of music on a scholarly level," and to serve as a billboard for upcoming musical events.

Keywords: music, classical, doctorate

Owner or Contact Bob Kosovsky, kos@cunyvms1.gc.cuny.edu, Theresa Muir, tfd@cunyvms1.gc.cuny.edu

To Subscribe E-mail LISTSERV@cunyvms1.gc.cuny.edu; in the body of the message, type **SUBSCRIBE CUNYMUS** followed by your real name. To unsubscribe, send the command **UNSUBSCRIBE CUNYMUS** in e-mail to LISTSERV@cunyvms1.gc.cuny.edu. Send all other list-related commands to LISTSERV@cunyvms1.gc.cuny.edu. For assistance, send the command **HELP**. Send all articles to CUNYMUS@cunyvms1.gc.cuny.edu.

Music Research

MUSIC-RESEARCH

Blending sciences and music, MUSIC-RESEARCH brings together musicologists, computer scientists, and others working on applications of computers in musicology and music analysis. I'm not sure what a "music representation system" is, but other discussions include information retrieval systems for musical scores, music printing for research applications, and computer applications in musicology and ethnomusicology.

Specifically not *discussed on* MUSIC-RESEARCH: *"Sound generation techniques, synthesizers, sequencers, or home music-making." Whew.*

Code D, M

Owner or Contact Stephen Page, sdpage@andersen.co.uk

To Subscribe Send a politely worded request to music-research-request@cat tell.psych.upenn.edu. To unsubscribe, send a politely worded request to music-research-request@cattell.psych.upenn.edu. Send all articles to MUSIC-RESEARCH@com lab.ox.ac.uk.

Upcoming Books, CDs, and Videos

BOOK-TALK

An up-to-the-minute source for soon-to-be-published books, CDs, and videos, including series titles from particular publishers, author discussions, pricing, availability, out-of-print titles, and subjects such as electronic publishing.

Though not specifically music-related, BOOK-TALK includes musical categories and is updated substantially with every list.

Code U (For a description of these codes, see "Mailing List Codes" in "Classical Music.")

Owner or Contact Paul Raulerson, paulr@columbia.ilc.com

To Subscribe E-mail LISTSERV@columbia.ilc.com; in the body of the message, type **SUBSCRIBE BOOK-TALK** followed by your real name. To unsubscribe, send the command **UNSUB BOOK-TALK** in e-mail to LISTSERV@columbia.ilc.com. Send all other list-related commands to LISTSERV@columbia.ilc.com. Send all articles to BOOK-TALK@columbia.ilc.com.

Appendices

Where Do I Go from Here?

Now that you know the basics and what's out there on the Internet, you may want to find out more about using the Internet. For example, you may want to learn in more detail about the World Wide Web, Usenet, Gopher, and FTP, *and* the software and tools you can use to make the most of your Internet travels. You may be interested in using the Net as a resource for improving your computer's musical playback capabilities, or for setting up your own favorite artist's Web page.

If you'd like a basic, plain English tour of the Internet and its uses, then *A Guided Tour of the Internet* by Christian Crumlish is for you. It's like having an Internet guru at your side, explaining everything as you go along. Another book for newbies is *Access the Internet* by David Peal. This book even includes NetCruiser software, which will get you connected via an easy point-and-click interface in no time.

For an introduction to the World Wide Web, turn to *Mosaic Access to the Internet* or *Surfing the Internet with Netscape*, both by Daniel A. Tauber and Brenda Kienan. Each of these books walks you through getting connected, and they both include the software you need to get started on the Web in a jiffy.

For quick and easy Internet reference, turn to the *Internet Instant Reference* by Paul Hoffman, and for an in-depth overview, try the best-selling *Internet Roadmap* by Bennett Falk. To get familiar with the lingo, you can turn to the compact and concise *Internet Dictionary* by Christian Crumlish.

If you've just got to learn all there is to know about the Internet, the comprehensive, *Mastering the Internet* by Glee Harrah Cady and Pat McGregor is for you. And if you want to find out what tools and utilities are available (often on the Internet itself) to maximize the power of your Internet experience, you'll want to check out *The Internet Tool Kit* by Nancy Cedeño.

All of these books have been published by Sybex in 1995 editions.

Internet Service Providers

If you're seeking an account with an Internet service provider, this appendix—which lists providers in the United States, Canada, Great Britain, Ireland, Australia, and New Zealand—is the place for you.

The service providers listed here offer full Internet service, *including SLIP/PPP accounts, which allow you to use Web browsers such as Mosaic and Netscape.*

The list provided here is by no means comprehensive, but rather one that concentrates on service providers that offer national or nearly national Internet service in English-speaking countries. To minimize your phone bill, you may prefer to use a local service provider, one who offers access via a local or toll-free phone number.

What's Out There

Two very good sources of information about Internet service providers are available on the Internet itself. Peter Kaminski's Public Dialup Internet Access list (PDIAL) is at ftp.netcom.com/pub/in/info-deli/public-access/pdial. Yahoo's Internet Access Providers list is at http://www.yahoo.com/Business/Corporations/Internet_Access_providers/.

When you inquire into establishing an account with any of the providers listed in this appendix, tell them the type of account you want. You may want a shell account (if you know and plan to use Unix commands to get around), or you may want the type of point-and-click access that's offered through Netcom's NetCruiser. If you want to run a Web browser like Mosaic or Netscape, you must have a SLIP or PPP account. Selecting an Internet service provider is a matter of personal preference and local access. Shop around, and if you aren't satisfied at any point, change providers.

When you're shopping around for an Internet service provider, the most important questions to ask are "What is the nearest local access number?" and "What are the monthly service charges?" Also ask if they charge a setup or registration fee.

IN THE UNITED STATES

In this section you'll find a list of Internet service providers that provide local access phone numbers in most major American cities. These are the large, national companies; many areas also have small regional Internet providers, which may offer better local access if you don't live in a big city. You can find out about these smaller companies by looking in local computer papers like *MicroTimes* or *Computer Currents* or by getting on the Internet via one of these big companies and checking out the Peter Kaminski and Yahoo service provider listings.

Opening an account with any of the providers listed here will get you full access to the World Wide Web, full-fledged e-mail service (allowing you to send and receive e-mail), and the ability to read and post articles to Usenet newsgroups.

Netcom Netcom Online Communications Services is a national Internet service provider with local access numbers in most major cities; as of this writing, they have 100 local access numbers in the United States. Netcom's NetCruiser software gives you point-and-click access to the Internet. (Netcom also provides a shell account, but stay away from it if you want to run Netscape.) Starting with NetCruiser version 1.6, it is possible to run Netscape on top of NetCruiser. Especially for beginning users who want a point-and-click interface and easy setup of Netscape, this may be a good choice.

NetCruiser software is available on disk for free at many trade shows and bookstores. It is also available bundled with David Peal's book *Access the Internet, Second Edition*, (Sybex, 1995), which shows you how to use the software. To contact Netcom directly, phone (800) 353-6600.

Performance Systems International Performance Systems International is a national Internet service provider with local access numbers in many American cities and in Japan. These folks are currently upgrading their modems to 28.8 kbps, which will give you faster access to the Internet.

To contact PSI directly, phone (800) 82P-SI82.

UUNet/AlterNet UUNet Technologies and AlterNet offer Internet service throughout the United States. They run their own national network.

You can contact UUnet and AlterNet at (800) 488-6383.

Portal Portal Communications, Inc., an Internet service provider located in the San Francisco Bay Area, lets you get connected either by dialing one of their San Francisco Bay Area phone numbers or via the CompuServe network. (This is not CompuServe Information Services, but rather the network on which CompuServe runs.) The CompuServe network, with over 400 access phone numbers, is a local call from most of the United States.

You can contact Portal at (408) 973-9111.

IN CANADA

Listed here are providers that offer access to Internet service in the areas around large Canadian cities. For information about local access in less populated regions, get connected and check out the Peter Kaminski and Yahoo lists described earlier in this appendix.

Many Internet service providers in the U.S. also offer service in Canada and in border towns near Canada. If you're interested (and you live in Canada), you can ask some of the big American service providers whether they have a local number near you.

UUNet Canada UUNet Canada is the Canadian division of the United States service provider UUNet/AlterNet, described earlier in this appendix. UUNet Canada offers Internet service to large portions of Canada.

You can contact UUNet Canada directly by phoning (416) 368-6621.

Internet Direct Internet Direct offers access to users in the Toronto and Vancouver areas.

You can contact Internet Direct by phoning (604) 691-1600 or faxing (604) 691-1605.

IN GREAT BRITAIN AND IRELAND

The Internet is, after all, international. Here are some service providers located and offering service in Great Britain and Ireland.

UNet Located in the northwest part of England, with more locations promised, UNet offers access at speeds up to 28.8 kbps, along with various Internet tools for your use.

They can be reached by phone at 0925 633 144.

Easynet London-based Easynet provides Internet service throughout England via Pipex, along with a host of Internet tools.

You can reach them by phone at 0171 209 0990.

Ireland On-Line Serving most (if not all) of Ireland, including Belfast, Ireland On-Line offers complete Internet service.

Contact Ireland On-Line by phone at 00 353 (0)1 8551740.

IN AUSTRALIA AND NEW ZEALAND

Music aficionados down under in Australia and New Zealand are as fascinated by the Internet as users in the northern hemisphere. Here are a couple of service providers for that part of the world.

Connect.com.au In Australia, Internet service via SLIP/PPP is available from Connect.com.au Pty Ltd.

You can contact them by phone at 61 3 528 2239.

Actrix Actrix Information Exchange offers Internet service (PPP accounts) in the Wellington, New Zealand area.

You can reach them by phone at 64 4 389 6316.

Index

Note to the Reader: Throughout this index **boldfaced** page numbers indicate primary discussions of a topic. *Italicized* page numbers indicate illustrations.